"I've Wanted to Hold You like This All Evening,"

Tyler confessed in a husky tone. In the privacy of the shadows, he took both of her arms and entwined them around his neck; then his own encircled her waist.

There was no obstacle between them now to prevent the growing awareness they had of each other. Impatient now, his mouth covered hers in a kiss that told her of desire and need long suppressed. His hands molded her hips to the outline of his body. Carly felt herself consumed by his passion, and yet it made her feel more alive than she had ever been in her entire life. . . .

SUZANNE SIMMS

was born in Storm Lake, Iowa, and currently resides in Indiana with her husband and nine-year-old son. She has a degree in English literature, loves opera, and studied classical piano for ten years. Ms. Simms loves reading and writing romances and believes being a successful romance writer is primarily a matter of attitude.

Dear Reader:

SILHOUETTE DESIRE is an exciting new line of contemporary romances from Silhouette Books. During the past year, many Silhouette readers have written in telling us what other types of stories they'd like to read from Silhouette, and we've kept these comments and suggestions in mind in developing SILHOUETTE DESIRE.

DESIREs feature all of the elements you like to see in a romance, plus a more sensual, provocative story. So if you want to experience all the excitement, passion and joy of falling in love, then SILHOUETTE DESIRE is for you.

I hope you enjoy this book and all the wonderful stories to come from SILHOUETTE DESIRE. I'd appreciate any thoughts you'd like to share with us on new SILHOUETTE DESIRE, and I invite you to write to us at the address below:

Karen Solem
Editor-in-Chief
Silhouette Books
P.O. Box 769
New York, N.Y. 10019

SUZANNE SIMMS
Moment In Time

Silhouette Desire
Published by Silhouette Books New York
America's Publisher of Contemporary Romance

SILHOUETTE BOOKS, a Simon & Schuster Division of
GULF & WESTERN CORPORATION
1230 Avenue of the Americas, New York, N.Y. 10020

ISBN: 0-671-44514-6

First Silhouette Books printing July, 1982

10 9 8 7 6 5 4 3 2 1

America's Publisher of Contemporary Romance

Printed in the U.S.A.

Moment
In Time

1

Mister Scott?" A gruff voice resounded through the small concourse.

Carlisle looked around the nearly deserted airport. There was an elderly woman, two men in business suits, and the man with the gruff voice. She took a step toward the man. "I'm *Miss* Scott."

"You the Carlyle Scott supposed to go out to Chula Vista this afternoon?"

"Yes, I am. It's the feminine spelling of Carlisle—C-A-R-L-I-S-L-E," she clarified for his benefit.

"Well, I'll be gawldurned if it ain't a female," drawled the man, as he pushed the Stetson back on his head. "Ou-eee!" The exclamation was part whoop, part laughter, all delivered in a low gravelly voice.

A voice and manner no doubt acquired by years on the

open range, the woman thought tongue in cheek, noting the faded denims and mud-encrusted boots.

"Boy, is Tyler gonna be surprised!"

"I beg your pardon," she responded, smoothing the skirt of her white linen suit.

"Begging your pardon, Miss Scott." The cowhand whipped off his hat and stood twisting it self-consciously in his hands. "It's just that we weren't expecting a lady—let alone one that looks like you do."

"I think I'll take that as a compliment, Mr.—ah . . ."

"Lew Hanken, ma'am, and I sure meant it as one."

"Mr. Hanken," she began, amused rather than angered, "my name has been confusing people for a long time. It started in grade school when I was mistakenly assigned a boy's locker in gym. So as you see, you aren't the first to make that mistake and you won't be the last."

Not by a long shot, she mused. She often used "Carly" now in her personal life, but tenaciously held to Carlisle professionally. Actually, as a civil engineer, it had come in handy on more than one occasion to have clients assume she was a man. Once they met her, however, there was no mistaking Carlisle Scott for a man. She was every inch a woman.

In the high heels she preferred to wear, Carlisle was taller than most of the male species. A happy circumstance in her opinion. She claimed to be five feet eight inches in height, but in truth was nearer to five seven. Her dark auburn hair was neatly coiled into some kind of bun arrangement at the back of her head. She believed the style provided her with an air of professionalism and credibility. Her eyes were hazel, or so it said on her driver's license, although their color did not fall into any one category.

Endowed with a well-proportioned body, which she neither took pains to conceal nor flaunt, she preferred tailored suits and neat little dresses for the office, practical but attractive pants for actual site operations.

Carlisle was wishing now she had chosen pants for this trip. The linen suit was already looking a little limp. "Shall we collect my luggage, Mr. Hanken? I'm rather anxious to reach Chula Vista."

"Yes, ma'am, follow me," he said, with a touch of deference.

They soon had her bags in hand and had made their way out of the Santa Fe airport.

"Sorry, Miss Scott," came the apology, as Lew Hanken quickly attempted to dust off the seat of the pickup truck with an equally dusty rag he obtained from under the seat. "If we'd known . . ." He looked bewilderedly from the white suit she was wearing to the still less than immaculate front seat.

"I assure you, Mr. Hanken, the life of an engineer is not one of luxury. Sometimes I think I've spent half my life in pickup trucks." As if to prove her point, Carlisle put a foot up and plunked herself down on the seat, dust and all, managing not to cringe at the thought of what it must be doing to her Evan Picone suit.

The man made short order of stowing her luggage in the rear and then they were under way. Carlisle slipped on a pair of designer sunglasses from her handbag and settled back as Lew Hanken maneuvered the truck out of the airport parking lot.

No community captured the essence of the Southwest better than Santa Fe, New Mexico, with its colorful blend of adobe and Spanish architecture, its fascinating past, and its rich mixture of Anglo, Indian, and Spanish-American cultures. Carlisle was aware Santa Fe was undergoing something of a rennaissance in the arts, and a friend had told her not to miss the unique shops that wound along Canyon Road. It was a shopper's dream to wander from one to the next, exploring the wares of potters, weavers, glassblowers, and artisans of every kind. She hoped to spend at least one weekend in the small high-plains city while she was here.

The pickup truck roughly gobbled up the miles as they headed east from Santa Fe and onto Highway 85, then north through the town of Las Vegas, New Mexico. Carlisle gazed out of the window at the sea of grass that stretched out on either side of the road. A range of purple mountains loomed on the horizon.

She turned to the man beside her. "What are those mountains, Mr. Hanken?" Despite the fact that Carlisle had lived in Denver, Colorado, for the past fifteen years, she had never lost her midwesterner's awe of mountains.

"Those are the Sangre de Cristos," he replied, then tacked on, apparently as an afterthought, "Get some pretty good thunderstorms up in them mountains."

Lew Hanken turned out to be a man of few words. The kind of man Carlisle could imagine having spent more than one night on the range with no one to talk to but his horse and a strong, bitter cup of coffee. His face was leathered to the same shade of brown his hair had no doubt once been. His gray eyes seemed to focus best when searching the horizon. It was impossible to guess his age.

Several miles down the road, the woman again attempted to engage him in conversation. "This part of New Mexico reminds me a little of Texas," she commented.

"Some call it 'Little Texas.'" He grunted. "Parts around here were settled when the cattlemen moved west from Texas after the Civil War."

"Chula Vista is a cattle ranch, isn't it?" Carlisle hoped that didn't sound too ignorant, but she knew so little about cattle.

"Yup!" Lew acknowledged, with his customary grunt.

"Just how big is Mr. Carson's ranch?" Never one to be easily put off, she persisted in her line of questioning.

The man stroked his chin for a moment before answering. "Hm—Tyler's got maybe fifty-two . . . fifty-three thousand acres. 'Course he runs cattle on another twenty-nine thousand acres of state land, too."

She gasped. "Why, that's huge!"

The ranch hand's throaty chuckle grated like a rusty nail against a strip of metal. "Naw! Back a few years . . ."—he chuckled again—". . . when I was a kid starting out, some of the big spreads ran to five hundred thousand acres. Could ride range all day and not see the end of them. *That* was big, Miss Scott."

"Yes," she murmured, as their conversation died of natural causes.

The pickup truck left the main highway and nosed down a dusty road that led out into the grassy plains. It was some time before Carlisle spotted a cluster of buildings in the distance.

"Chula Vista," the man announced, with a perfunctory nod of his head.

As they pulled up in front of the ranch house, Carlisle feasted her eyes on the trim two-story adobe. She had expected to see adobe architecture here in New Mexico, but the riotous burst of color provided by the carefully tended flower beds was a breathtaking surprise. An archway led to a picturesque courtyard beyond, a wishing well at its center.

"Here, I'll take that," she offered, as she let herself out of the pickup and took the smallest of her bags from the man. With a handbag slung over her shoulder, a briefcase in one hand and a suitcase in the other, it was quite a load. Lew Hanken followed her with two larger pieces of luggage.

They had nearly reached the front door when it swung open and a middle-aged woman of indeterminate years came bustling out to meet them. She had nary a hair out of place, her apron—Carlisle hadn't thought anyone still wore aprons—was clean and crisp, and only the slightest flicker of her blue eyes registered surprise when Lew Hanken introduced Carlisle as their expected guest.

The woman extended a friendly smile and a handshake. "Welcome to Chula Vista, Miss Scott. I'm Rosemary Quinn, Tyler's housekeeper. Glad you made it here all in one piece. I see you took that old pickup, after all." She addressed the latter to Lew in a loudly exaggerated voice, as if he were hard of hearing.

"Now, Rosemary . . ." the man placated, "I got her here safe and sound, didn't I?"

Carlisle forced herself not to smile at the exchange

between the burly cowboy and the rather diminutive housekeeper.

"Well, as long as you're here you may as well make yourself useful and take the young lady's things upstairs," the woman said with a sniff. "Put them in the back bedroom. The one in the southwest corner. It'll have to do for now."

Carlisle turned her attention to the man behind them for a moment. "Thank you for meeting me at the airport, Mr. Hanken."

"You're welcome, miss," he mumbled, busying himself with her luggage.

"Come along then, Miss Scott," the housekeeper urged. "You must be tired after your trip." Without actually taking her guest by the arm, she guided the younger woman into the house.

The interior of the ranch house was as neat and tidy as Rosemary Quinn herself, if that were possible. The floors were covered with area rugs in muted earth shades, the adobe walls sparingly accented with western prints and works of Indian art. A large God's-eye covered one wall of the entranceway as a dramatic introduction. The furniture appeared to be antique and of excellent quality, but comfortable-looking and lived-in as well. Carlisle managed only a glimpse here and there as she trotted along behind the housekeeper. She had to admit it was far more civilized than she had expected and found she looked forward to exploring the house in greater depth if and when the opportunity presented itself.

"Would you care for a cool drink, Miss Scott, and perhaps a bite to eat? I never know if Tyler will be in early or late, so dinner is usually around eight o'clock. You might want something to tide you over. I baked an angel food cake fresh this morning," she went on to offer.

"It sounds delicious, Mrs. Quinn, but . . ."

"Please, make that 'Rosemary,'" the woman interjected. "We don't stand on formalities in this house."

"In that case, if you don't mind, Rosemary, I would like to freshen up a bit first," Carlisle replied, glancing down at the brown streaks that creased the front of her white skirt.

"Of course," she readily agreed, leading the way up the staircase and along the hallway to the last bedroom. "I would have put you in Dorothy's old room—that's Tyler's sister—if I'd known." The woman apologized in tone, if not in words. "I'm afraid this one is more to a man's liking." Rosemary opened the door and stepped aside for Carlisle to enter.

"But it's a lovely bedroom," she reassured the housekeeper, upon seeing the big double bed with handwoven spread and rich wine-colored carpet. The furniture was a dark-grained wood, perhaps pine, and rather massive in proportions, but Carlisle had never been one for a lot of lace and frills, anyway. "I'm sure I will be very comfortable here."

Rosemary Quinn briskly stepped forward. "The bathroom is through that door and this is the closet. I put out fresh linens, but if you need anything else, just ask. You come on down to the kitchen whenever you're good and ready. I'll have something for you."

"Thank you. You've been most kind," Carlisle murmured as the woman took her leave, closing the bedroom door behind her.

With a wistful look at the beckoning expanse of bed, the young woman put the idea of a nap from her mind and began to unpack only the barest essentials. There was no sense in unpacking any more than that. She would no doubt be moving up to the construction site first thing in the morning. Her clothes could simply stay as they were.

Living out of a suitcase as she had virtually done for the past few years had taught Carlisle to buy wrinkle-free clothing and how to pack so it stayed that way. One day when she had the time she would write a "how to" guide for the traveling woman. She certainly possessed the background for it, although she had to plead temporary insanity for wearing a white linen suit today.

The young woman stepped out of her clothes and within minutes was blissfully washing the dust and grime from her body. She reveled in the pulsating spray of steamy water that pelted her skin, turning her a delicious pink all over. It was the one luxury she missed most while working on a site operation. There, showers were hurried affairs and the water lukewarm at best.

Carlisle toweled off and quickly dressed in a perky little sundress with an embroidered bodice. She freshened her hairdo and makeup, and while both were flattering to her, she made certain they could be maintained with a minimum of fuss. Her one bow to vanity was the long sheath of auburn hair that tumbled to the middle of her back when it was allowed to flow free. She refused to have it cut in a short cropped style and resorted to the traditional bun instead.

Once she was ready and had tidied her room, Carlisle sat down on the edge of the bed and opened her briefcase. She was particularly anxious to get to work on this project. Although Warren Taylor, the engineer originally assigned to this job, had been thorough in his preliminary reports, she wanted to see the dam site for herself. She had all of Warren's notes and detailed plans, but would feel better once she had checked them to her own satisfaction.

This was by no means the biggest project Carlisle had tackled. In fact, it was one of the smaller—in size, anyway. But it was a project of vision and purpose that had appealed to her father as head of the engineering firm. He was concerned with proper water management, so vital to the future of the Southwest. When he was approached by Tyler Carson on behalf of a small group of ranchers from northeastern New Mexico to construct a dam on an offshoot of the Canadian River, Thomas Scott had agreed for his firm to take on the job.

"Enough!" Carlisle put the papers away and snapped the briefcase closed. She wandered across the bedroom to a glass door that apparently led to some kind of terrace beyond and stood looking out.

"I wonder what you will think, Mr. Tyler Carson , when you discover a woman engineer has been assigned to build your precious dam," she thought aloud.

Well, she was a damned good engineer! A better engineer than Warren Taylor, if the truth were told. Her father had asked her to take over this project as a personal favor to him, and Carlisle had readily agreed for several reasons—not the least of which was that it provided the perfect break she needed from Richard.

Dear sweet Richard—she did enjoy his urbane company, but of late he had become increasingly persistent, despite her rebuffs. Like the majority of men, Richard thought he should be the beginning, middle, and end of a woman's interest. Despite his denials Carlisle knew he considered his own career more important than hers. There could be no future for her with any man who thought that way.

Men! She shook her head and with that in mind her thoughts strayed back to her host. Actually, she knew very little of the man. Warren had seemed singularly impressed by him and his dedication to the future of New Mexico. What she knew of Tyler Carson beyond that could be ticked off on one hand. He was a cattle rancher in his mid-thirties and reportedly unmarried. It wasn't much to go on, but then meetings between the two of them would be infrequent and strictly business.

A low grumbling from the pit of her stomach signaled that it was time she took Rosemary Quinn up on the offer of refreshments. With a final check of her appearance in the mirror she made her way downstairs.

There were no signs of life anywhere, but recalling the housekeeper's admonishment against formality, she boldly ventured along the hallway to the rear of the house. There at the end of the hall she did indeed find the kitchen—but that was not all Carlisle Scott found!

"Good Lord!" she muttered, under her breath. "What do we have here?"

For hunched over a wooden bench by the back door was the dustiest, dirtiest cowboy she had ever seen—not that Carlisle had seen many. Unaware of her presence, at least for the moment, the man continued to pull his boots

17

off and set them on an old newspaper on the floor. Next his hat was removed and expertly tossed onto a hook by the screen door. As he straightened up, one hand already undoing the buttons of his shirt, he caught sight of Carlisle out of the corner of his eye.

The man slowly turned to face her, his eyes raking her body from top to bottom in typically male fashion. She wordlessly endured the once-over inflicted on her by this arrogant cowboy with manure on his boots and a glaze of dust on his skin and clothing, aware of the faint but unmistakable aroma of cattle that had come into the kitchen with him. His brown hair was matted on his forehead as if he had worn a sweaty Stetson all day. His eyes were large and dark with squint lines at the corners. The larger-than-life features had been drawn by a bold, dauntless hand.

Whoever he was, he was not much the taller of the two. Carlisle was wearing her usual high-heeled sandals while the man stood there in his socks. It should have put him at a disadvantage, but somehow it didn't work out that way.

"Well . . . hello!" The cultured, if sensual, baritone came as a complete surprise. "It seems our engineer has brought a 'companion' with him. Come here, honey, so I can get a good look at you. I'm not allowed beyond this point in work clothes."

"I'd say you've already had a good look, mister," she ground the R between her teeth.

The man went on talking as though he hadn't heard a word she'd said. "Funny, you don't look like a secretary. . . ."

"That's because I'm not." Carlisle held on to her

temper, imploring the fates to let this cowboy dig the hole just a little deeper.

The man's fingers unconsciously rumpled the hair plastered to his head. "You know, I don't seem to recall any mention in Scott's letter that he was bringing someone with him." There was just the slightest hesitancy in his voice.

"*She* didn't." Each word exploded in the silence of the room like a small bomb. It was a moment to relish.

"*You're* Carlisle Scott?" said the man.

"And you must be Tyler Carson." She could have kicked herself for not realizing who he was sooner. "Any relation to Kit?" she flippantly tossed out.

His laughter was spontaneous. "As a matter of fact, Kit Carson lived in this part of New Mexico, over by Taos. Everybody claims to be related in some way to the legendary scout." Tyler had turned and pulled off the cotton work shirt as he spoke.

In spite of the dirt and grime smeared across his chest, the woman couldn't help but notice the rippling well-developed muscles that flexed when he moved. "Whipcord" was the word that sprang to mind. Carlisle knew she was staring, but she couldn't seem to take her eyes off the man. Tyler Carson was without a doubt one of the finest physical specimens she had ever seen.

"Now—if you will excuse me, Miss Scott—I need a shower and a change of clothes."

She wrinkled up her nose. "I wouldn't dream of stopping you, Mr. Carson." She had glimpsed what appeared to be a bathroom and some kind of office behind him and assumed this was his destination.

The man continued to undress. First he removed his

socks, then the leather belt that hugged his hips. When he got to the zipper of his jeans, he hesitated. "Of course, you're welcome to stay, Miss Scott, but . . ."

"Excuse me, Mr. Carson." With Tyler's laughter ringing in her ears, Carlisle made a hasty retreat from the kitchen. He may only have been teasing her, but she was not about to take a chance and call his bluff. Suddenly the humor of the situation hit her. The man really was impossible, she chuckled, but then men so often were.

She was still smiling as she strolled down the front hall to the living room. With little else to occupy her time, she poked her nose in here and there and soon found herself admiring the house if not the man. Row upon row of books covered one wall from ceiling to floor. While Carlisle wasn't surprised by the wide range of titles on New Mexico, she was puzzled by the disproportionate number of law books.

She moved on, studying the collection of arrowheads and other artifacts mounted above the fireplace. Richly textured rugs and colorful hand-thrown pottery were a natural extension of the room's western decor. A brightly painted kachina doll was on display in a niche in the wall itself. Yet the overall impression was one of a home with carefully preserved family treasures. Carlisle was certain a decorator's hand had had no part in it.

Sometime later she became aware that she was no longer alone in the room. She didn't know what it was that made her turn around, but she wasn't in the least surprised to see Tyler Carson propped against the arched doorway watching her.

The transformation in the man's appearance nearly

brought a gasp to her lips. Gone was the rustic cowboy she had encountered in the kitchen—here was a suave, sophisticated man of the world. A regular Dr. Jekyll and Mr. Hyde, Carlisle thought. His hair was a lighter shade of brown than she had originally suspected, the skin a golden bronze and surprisingly smooth in appearance. He wore a pair of dark brown trousers that hugged his muscular thighs and a blue silk shirt left open at the neck. She found herself wondering why golden men always looked more golden in that particular shade of blue.

He continued studying her until she felt decidedly uncomfortable and rather warm in the face. "T-this is a lovely room," she stammered. "Someone has collected some interesting and beautiful pieces."

"It started with my great-grandmother," Tyler replied, his gaze leaving her for the first time since entering the room. "The kachina was hers. Most of the other things belonged to my grandfather or my parents." He gestured toward the collection mounted over the rounded fireplace. "I found the arrowheads when I was a kid."

"Did you?" She didn't know why that would surprise her. Even Tyler Carson had to have been a boy once.

"Yes, my grandfather was something of an amateur archaeologist and I would tag along whenever he'd let me. He had quite a collection at one time. Most of it is in a museum down by Santa Fe now." His tone conveyed a shrug.

The woman pointed to a spot on the wall above his head. "That one is different from the others, isn't it?"

"Actually, that's not an arrowhead but a prehistoric stone spearhead called a 'Folsom point.' When the first one was unearthed about sixty years ago, it was an indication that Indians hunted in this area at least ten thousand years ago. But I think that's enough history for your first evening here, Miss Scott, don't you?" His mouth twitched at the corners. "Rosemary said dinner would be ready in a few minutes. She seemed particularly concerned about you." The brown eyes flickered humorously. "She must be to have dinner ready this early. Shall we?" The man extended his arm to her.

Carlisle bit her tongue and graciously accepted his offer. "By all means, Mr. Carson—lead on."

Dinner was a traditional steak-and-potatoes meal which Carlisle thoroughly enjoyed. She had always had a hearty appetite and tonight was no exception. Conversation was brisk as each in turn tried to score off the other. It was more a heated tennis match than a dinnertime tête-à-tête, but somewhere between the salad and steak a truce was declared and the remainder of the meal passed uneventfully.

Carlisle sighed and put her fork down. While there might be a certain exhilaration in matching wits with a man like Tyler Carson, it was exhausting, as well. At twenty-nine she knew enough of human psychology to recognize the undertones to their verbal jousting. Only a fool could have missed it. It had been there, too, in the surreptitious glances they had exchanged over the steak and baked potatoes. Tyler had obviously been feeling out his opponent's strengths and weaknesses just as she had been.

The woman shook her head as if to clear away the cobwebs spun by the two—or had it been three—glasses of sangría? She really should have been counting. After all, she was here to do a job, not to socialize. Straightening her spine against the hard chair-back, she turned to her host.

"I'm sure you can understand my position, Mr. Carson, I am most anxious to see the dam site for myself." She tried to sound very businesslike.

"Why don't you make it 'Tyler'?" The man leaned forward and took her hand in his, simply oozing with charm.

Carlisle's train of thought was effectively broken. "All right—Tyler." She jerked her hand back. "I want to move on location as soon as possible, preferably first thing tomorrow."

"We may have a bit of a problem there." He was hedging and they both knew it. "The accommodations made were for a male engineer, as you may have guessed. Since you are definitely a female . . ."

"I want no special amenities because I'm a woman," she said coolly. "I am quite sure that whatever arrangements were made for Warren Taylor will be suitable."

"No doubt the two men with whom the engineer was supposed to bunk will be delighted to hear that," he retorted. "This is a small operation, Carlisle. We don't have the facilities to provide you with your own trailer."

"Very well." She reluctantly conceded the point. To do otherwise would be churlish. "Then perhaps you could tell me where the nearest hotel is?"

The man shook his head as if he thought she had gotten a bit too much sun. "In case you hadn't noticed, this isn't exactly a metropolitan area. The only practical alternative is for you to stay here. I'll make sure you have a vehicle at your disposal each morning to commute to the site." Tyler leaned back as if that settled the matter.

"I'll be here all summer building that dam. I wouldn't dream of presuming on your hospitality."

"It's the least I can do. After all, there's plenty of room here, and my ranch will reap the major benefits from the construction of the dam."

"No—I couldn't possibly stay here that long. If you won't help me then I'll have to make other arrangements on my own." Carlisle absently fingered the napkin on her lap.

"When will you get it through that lovely head of yours that there are no other suitable arrangements that can be made?" Tyler failed to conceal his annoyance with her. "It's not as if you would be alone in the house with me, if that's what's bothering you. Rosemary is always here, too."

"No, that's not it, of course," she said disdainfully. Yet the idea of living in such close proximity with the man for weeks on end, even with a housekeeper ensconced on the first floor, spelled trouble in her book.

Tyler took a long draw on the small cigar he had lit. "Then it's settled—you'll stay here."

"At least for the time being," she added with caution.

The man reached for the coffeepot at his elbow. "Would you like a refill?"

"Yes, please." Carlisle held out her cup.

"Look, I wouldn't want you to take this wrong, but let me give you a piece of friendly advice." Tyler looked her straight in the eyes. "Most of the workmen you will be dealing with on this project have never had a female boss before, let alone one as beautiful as you are. Go a little easy on the buddy-buddy stuff, at least at the beginning."

Carlisle felt the blood rush to her face. How dare this—this *cowboy* tell *her* how she should conduct herself! "I assure you, Mr. Carson," she breathed through her teeth, "that I behave in a professional manner at all times."

He dismissed her statement. "I'm sure you do, but there are certain cultural differences here you may not have dealt with before. Some of the crew don't speak English as their first language, for example. Some things might be better left to your foreman, who is fluent in Spanish as well as the predominant Indian dialect."

"While I appreciate your concern"—it was obvious she did not—"may I remind you that I have worked as a civil engineer for the past eight years and before that I spent four years in classrooms filled almost exclusively with men. I could hardly be a stranger to the male mentality under the circumstances." Her coffee cup clattered in the saucer.

"So 'Miss Confidence,' you think you've run into it all?"

"There isn't a line I haven't heard, a ploy that hasn't been tried on me at least a dozen times. Believe me, I'll manage. I always have before and I will this time, too. Sooner or later the fact that I'm a damned good professional gets through to my crews." Carlisle paused for a much needed breath. "And may I further remind you that the engineer originally assigned to this project spoke not one word of Spanish or Indian dialect either. Apparently you didn't feel it was going to be a problem for him. I do have enough sense to use the resources at my disposal." She grabbed her cup and took a gulp, not thinking that it had been refilled with very hot coffee. "Oh!" Carlisle reached for a glass of cold water and quickly took a drink.

"Are you all right?" Tyler's voice was sharp with concern.

"Yes, I'll be fine," she whispered a little hoarsely.

"Look, all I'm saying is that some of the men may not take kindly to a woman being in charge."

"Perhaps not—or perhaps the prejudice you so eloquently express on their behalf is actually your own. Perhaps it is *you*, Mr. Carson, who would not 'take kindly' to a female boss. Or is it because you're an Anglo? Maybe your ideas about people from other cultural backgrounds is a little distorted. Either way, I assure you, sir, your dam will be built!"

She watched with fascination as a red-hot flush moved up the man's neck and into his face.

"Don't pass judgment on things you know nothing about, Miss Scott." So they were that quickly back to "Mr. Carson" and "Miss Scott." "Now if you will excuse me, I have some paperwork that needs my attention." The anger still raw in his voice and manner, Tyler abruptly rose from his chair and left the dining room.

After his departure, Carlisle fell limp against the table, every emotion wrung from her body. She wasn't usually so quick to take offense, or give it for that matter. But there was something about this man that put her back up. She slowly got up and began to stack their dishes on the serving cart.

"There, there, I'll be doing that," Rosemary insisted as

she appeared from the kitchen. "You must be exhausted. Why not go on up to your room?"

"I think I will." Carlisle wearily drew a hand across her eyes. "I guess I am tired at that."

"Sure you are—traveling all day and being in a strange place besides. You try to get a good night's rest."

"Thank you, I will. By the way, your dinner was delicious."

The woman was obviously pleased by the compliment. "Wasn't anything special, but I'm glad you enjoyed it," she responded, finishing up the job Carlisle had begun.

"Well, good night then, Rosemary."

"See you in the morning, dearie," the housekeeper called out after her.

Every step was a concerted effort as the young woman made her way upstairs to her bedroom. She went through the routine of preparing for bed, suddenly too tired to think or care of anything beyond sleep. She even skipped the nightly brushing she usually gave her hair, content to simply take out the bobby pins, and with a shake of her head, allow it to tumble to her shoulders in a mass of auburn waves.

Carlisle climbed between the fragrant sheets and reached for the bedside lamp just as a knock came at the door. She pulled the covers up around her before answering. "Yes?"

The door opened to admit Tyler Carson. "I just stopped in to say good night," he explained, his eyes dark and unreadable in the faint light. "Is the room comfortable?"

"The room is fine, thank you."

"Ah, look, Carlisle," he said, getting to the real reason for his nocturnal visit. "I know I was pretty heavy-handed with you earlier, but dammit, you're a beautiful woman and that complicates matters whether you like it or not! You can't stay at the site. Surely you can see that? It's pretty remote around here. In this part of New Mexico there are fewer than three people per square mile. Hell, we've got twice as many sheep and cattle in this state as we do people!"

That brought a smile to Carlisle's lips in spite of herself. "Then I'll be sure to watch out for the sheep and cattle."

"My warning referred to the two-legged variety of animal, as you well know," he stated in a gruff voice, but he, too, was grinning now. "Believe me, I know what I'm talking about." Tyler's voice grew infinitely softer. "God knows, you look like a warm, inviting woman with your hair down around your shoulders. It would tempt the most honorable man to run his hands through its silky fire."

Their laughter seemed to die away of some mutual accord, leaving in its wake an almost tangible thread of awareness. An awareness Carlisle recognized had existed between them from that first moment in the kitchen. The intimacy of the bedroom and her state of undress only served to heighten the impression. If Tyler Carson were any kind of man—and he was—he had to be cognizant of it as well.

Unlike the indifference she had adopted toward most men, Carlisle was all too physically aware of this one. She even found herself wondering if he were going to make a pass at her. Surely at her age she could handle whatever came her way, even from a man like Tyler—if she chose to.

"You should wear your hair like that more often," he murmured, his gaze brushing her face.

Carlisle answered before thinking. "I do at night."

"I'll have to remember that," he exhaled on a long breath. "Well, I'll say good night then." His hand went to the doorknob. "See you in the morning . . . and pleasant dreams."

Carlisle reached for the bedside lamp and clicked it off. The night seemed to mount around her. "You, too, Tyler," she said quietly.

"I'm sure I will," the man muttered under his breath. "I'm sure I will."

2

Carlisle awoke early the next morning. The dazzling brilliance of the New Mexico sun poured in through the window, flooding the bedroom with a golden light. She quickly dressed in rugged chinos and one of the two pairs of hiking boots she had brought with her. She applied a special moisturizer under her makeup. A woman in her line of work soon learned to take sensible precautions if she did not wish to end up looking like a dried prune. With her long hair pinned up, she pulled on a jaunty little brimmed cap to further protect her skin and hair from the sun. Carlisle didn't wish to foster the idea of a glamour girl playing at being an engineer, but neither did she want to deliberately appear unattractive.

When she came down to the kitchen for breakfast she found that Tyler Carson had already gone. He must have been up before dawn.

"How about steak and eggs for breakfast?" Rosemary Quinn asked with a cheery smile. "You need a good hearty meal to start the day with the kind of work you do."

"Oh, I couldn't ask you to cook another whole meal just for me. I didn't realize Tyler would be up so early."

"I don't mind. Goodness, I used to cook for a crew of a dozen back when my husband was living. Kind of miss not having someone to fuss over." The woman turned away, but not before Carlisle saw the teary eyes that had nothing to do with the onions the housekeeper was chopping.

"Did your husband work for Tyler?"

"Land sakes, no, dear, he worked for Tyler's father. Why I can remember Tyler's grandparents and even the old lady, his great-grandmother. I was a bride when Frank came to work at Chula Vista. Had ourselves a real nice bungalow a couple of miles down the road. One egg or two?" Rosemary interrupted herself to take Carlisle's order for breakfast.

"One, please."

The housekeeper expertly cracked the egg with one hand while she threw a thick steak into the iron skillet with the other. "After I lost Frank, Tyler's mother asked me if I'd like to move up here to the big house. Tyler was away at college then, but Dorothy was still at home. I liked being part of a family. Been here almost fifteen years now, but the house seems kind of empty with Tyler the only one who lives in it permanent. I'd like to see him married, children in the house again. . . ." The woman set a heaping plate of food in front of Carlisle. "You married dear?"

31

"No, I'm not." She coughed, trying to choke back her laughter. No one could accuse Rosemary Quinn of subtlety, not that Carlisle was offended by the question. An unmarried woman of her age was considered fair game by every matchmaking aunt and well-meaning friend who came along. She had learned to view the whole subject with a sense of humor, for the sake of her sanity if for no other reason.

The housekeeper poured herself a cup of coffee and sat down at the kitchen table. "By the way, Tyler asked me to tell you he'll be back to take you up to the dam site, seeing how it's your first day and all."

"Oh . . ." The fork in Carlisle's hand stopped in midair. "I didn't expect him to go to any trouble for me."

"He's a thoughtful man that Tyler—when he puts his mind to it. Got a lot of responsibility on his shoulders running a place like this. He needs a good woman by his side, not some chit of a girl who fancies herself playing mistress of the manor." The woman gave one good nod of her head.

"Yes, I suppose so," Carlisle mumbled. It was the first critical comment she had heard the housekeeper make and couldn't help but wonder if she had anyone in particular in mind.

"There aren't many chances for Tyler to meet the right kind of woman with the hours he works. Doesn't have enough fun if you ask me." She sniffed.

"I can't imagine women being a problem for a man as attractive as Tyler Carson," the younger woman admitted begrudgingly.

For some unknown reason this brought a broad smile

to the housekeeper's face. "Well, I better let you finish your breakfast," she said, getting to her feet.

Carlisle Scott did exactly that and then retired to the living room to once more go over Warren Taylor's analysis of the site's formation and stream-flow characteristics, although she nearly had the information committed to memory. It was what she loved best about her work—putting all the pieces together like a jigsaw puzzle and creating something in the process. She was so engrossed she did not hear the man return, nor was she aware of his presence until he spoke.

"Ready to go to work this morning, Miss Scott?"

"Certainly, Mr. Carson." She stuffed the papers back in her briefcase and scrambled to her feet, only to discover the man was standing so close to her she could scarcely breathe without bumping into the muscled wall of his chest. Carlisle stood there for a moment, the back of her knees painfully pressed into the chair. Her eyes took in the jeans riding low on his hips, the blue serge work shirt, the leather vest, and finally, the handsome face watching her.

"So—this is what our lady engineer looks like when she's off to build a dam." Tyler seemed intrigued. Then he gave her cap a brotherly tug. "Let's go, shall we?"

"Yes." She breathed easier once he stepped back to let her pass.

Once they were outside, Carlisle saw the Jeep parked by the back door. She was about to put a foot up to climb into the passenger side when Tyler interceded. "You drive," he said, tossing her a set of keys. "Head west down that road until I tell you differently."

"Yessir!" she smartly answered.

For the first few miles Carlisle concentrated wholly on her driving. She hadn't been this nervous behind the wheel since her first road test at sixteen. It was all her own silly fault, too. Tyler hadn't said or done anything to make her feel self-conscious. In fact, with one leg nonchalantly propped against the dash, the Stetson pushed back off his face, he looked like he was going out for a joyride.

"This dam is going to make a big difference to the ranchers around here, Carlisle," he finally said.

"Yes, I know. That's why the firm agreed to build it," she shouted over the roar of the Jeep.

Tyler Carson turned around and casually put an arm on the back of the driver's seat. A harmless gesture in itself, but it brought to Carlisle's attention the fact that a mere inch or two separated the lean male body from her own. His breath wafted warm against her cheek as he spoke.

"Tom Scott is the head of the firm, isn't he?"

She nodded her head. "Yes—he is." Unknowingly her face and voice softened at the mention of the dear lovable man who was her boss as well as her father.

The man beside her sat back and looked out across the plains. "Are you married, Carlisle?"

At first she thought he was just teasing her. After all, he had been calling her "Miss Scott" for two days now. Then Carlisle convinced herself she must have heard him incorrectly. "W-what did you say?"

"Are—you—married?" Tyler repeated in a louder voice, enunciating each word as if it were a dagger.

"T-that's what I thought you said," she stammered. "No, I'm not married."

"You're not?"

"No!" What in the world did it take to convince him of that? And why was everyone so interested in her marital status, or lack of it? Tyler was the second person to cross-examine her on the subject this morning and it wasn't even eight o'clock yet!

The rancher inched closer. "Then Tom Scott is your . . ."

". . . father." She finished the sentence for him.

"Of course!" Carlisle wheeled at the sound of his laughter. "Turn right up ahead." He grinned.

She shook her head, questioning in her mind the mental stability of the man next to her. Perhaps he as well as Lew Hanken had spent too many solitary nights out on the range.

When they reached the crest of the next hill, Carlisle did not have to be told they had arrived at their destination. There ahead was a small narrow canyon and the river running like liquid silver between its stone walls. Men and machinery were busily milling about as they set up camp. She pulled in next to the first trailer and jumped out of the Jeep. This moment of beginning always sent a thrill through her veins. It did no less this time.

Two men separated from the crowd and came toward them as Tyler stepped out. "Bill . . . Phillip," he smiled, grasping each by the hand in greeting.

Carlisle saw curiosity light in both pairs of male eyes as she walked around to the front of the Jeep. It was no less than she had expected under the circumstances. Naturally these men were wondering what she was doing here. But curiosity was quickly replaced by something more—a kind of cool sexual appraisal—on the part of the one Tyler had called Phillip. It was a look she had seen before and it usually meant trouble sooner or later.

Evidently she was not the only one to have seen it. In a deliberate move, Tyler Carson slipped an arm about her waist and drew her forward for the introductions. "Honey, this is Bill Montoya, your foreman, and Phil Thompson, the architect. Gentlemen, the engineer on this project—Carlisle Scott."

"Hello." She smiled and gave each man a firm handshake, trying her best to ignore the proprietary arm around her waist, an arm that somehow said "hands off—she's mine." Carlisle had a fairly good idea why Tyler had done it, but she required no man's protection and she intended to inform him of that fact the moment they were alone. She was quite capable of fighting her own battles, thank you. "I'll just get my briefcase and then we can get to work." She stepped back to the Jeep, only to find Tyler right there beside her.

"Now don't be angry, honey," he spoke close to her ear. Carlisle could detect the amusement in his voice, feel his chest shaking with laughter. It made her all the angrier.

"Don't you *honey* me, Tyler Carson!" Each word was clipped and staccato.

"I did it for a reason, Carlisle. By the way, those are the two men you were supposed to bunk with," he interjected. "I'm not concerned about Bill, but Phillip Thompson has something of a reputation as a ladies' man. I simply thought we'd take care of that problem before it began. If Phil suspects there's something between us, he won't have the guts to bother you."

"Why not? Does he think you'll beat him up?" she asked half in jest.

"Something like that." He was perfectly serious.

Carlisle rolled her eyes heavenward. "Good grief—it's the wild wild West, after all."

"No sense in inviting trouble if you can avoid it. I think Phil will behave himself now."

She put an exasperated hand on her hip and cocked her head toward Tyler. "Gee . . . I don't know how I got along without you all these years," she said, sarcasm richly lacing her voice.

"Neither do I," he came back smartly.

Carlisle deduced that it was next to impossible to stay mad at this man, but she faced him squarely nonetheless. "Look, don't do me any more favors, all right?"

"Yes, ma'am," he drawled, with a lazy, infuriating smile. "You just go on about your business. I want to say hello to some of the men I know working on the project."

"Men!" she mumbled, retrieving her briefcase from the back of the Jeep and rejoining Bill Montoya and a rather subdued Phil Thompson.

But her eyes followed the figure making its way across the rugged terrain. She watched Tyler work the group of men like an accomplished politician would a crowd. No, that was more of an insult than a compliment these days. He was greeted as a respected leader, a trusted friend, knowing most of them by name and even asking about their families. With one he switched to Spanish, apparently speaking the language quite well. To another he mumbled in a dialect Carlisle was totally unacquainted with. She turned to Bill Montoya. "What language was Tyler speaking just now?"

"Tewa."

"Tewa?" It didn't mean anything to her.

"Tewa is the dialect of the Taos Pueblos," he explained. "There are nineteen Pueblos in New Mexico, but our people are all of a common ancestry. Although we speak different dialects, they are related. Tyler has always believed that diverse cultures and languages should be kept alive. The men feel a certain honor in being addressed in their own language by a man like Tyler." The affection and respect in Bill's voice showed he believed it to be true.

"It's a wonder he hasn't been pressed into a political career," she observed wryly, all the while admiring the man's style. Tyler certainly had what they called "charisma" back in Speech 200 during her freshman year of college.

"Believe me, they've tried, but Tyler has his own ideas about his role in helping New Mexico—and it isn't through politics."

"Have you known him a long time?"

"All of my life," he answered without hesitation, as they watched Tyler Carson walk back toward them. Then a thunderous pounding of hooves behind them drew their attention elsewhere. It was Lew Hanken mounted on horseback, a large palomino in tow.

"Better come take her, Tyler. She hasn't taken kindly to second place behind Lady," the cowboy called out.

With a final tip of his Stetson in salute, the man swung up into the saddle. "See you back at the house for dinner, Carlisle. Keep an eye on her, Bill—she's a live one!"

For just a moment the rider and golden horse seemed as one. Carlisle found her heart beating like a ceremonial drum. If there were any doubts in her mind that Tyler Carson was unlike any man she had ever met, they vanished in that moment.

"Let's get to work," she addressed the two men beside her as the horses disappeared over the hill. "I'd like to walk the site first thing. I've gone over Warren Taylor's notes and I have an idea we may be able to save ourselves some time and work by drilling through the adjacent canyon wall here." She unrolled the map under her arm and pointed to a spot she had marked. Then there was no time to think of the disturbing Tyler Carson, not that day, anyway.

Dusk was already sweeping across the mountains and onto the plains when Carlisle Scott drove back to the ranch house. It had been a rough first day in some respects, but then first days often were rough, she reminded herself. At least the crew and equipment had shown up without any apparent hitches and excavation was scheduled to begin the following morning. She spent the remainder of the drive calculating whether she needed another tracked excavator to do the job properly.

Carlisle parked the Jeep at the rear of the adobe ranch house. Mindful of Rosemary Quinn's penchant for tidiness, she paused inside the kitchen door long enough to remove her boots. That was when she spotted the dusty cowboy boots already in place on the neatly folded newspaper. Evidently Tyler had made it back for dinner before her.

She straightened up and wearily made her way upstairs, planning no further ahead than the wonderfully cool shower that awaited her. There were times when Carlisle wondered why she did it—working month after month on a project from sunup to sundown. She was seriously thinking of taking an extended vacation after this one and could well afford to, what with the nice nest egg she had put away for herself. But didn't she always tell herself that at the beginning and end of every project?

With scarcely a thought for what she was doing, Carlisle undressed and slipped into a short kimono-style robe. She had intended to take her shower first thing, but the temptation to stretch out on the bed for a few minutes proved too great to resist. She set her alarm clock for precisely half an hour and flopped down on the bed without even bothering to pull back the spread. She was asleep within seconds.

It took wave upon wave of nearly icy shower water to bring her to life again, but eventually a feeling of being human returned. Carlisle chose a deceptively simple dress from her closet to wear for dinner that evening. The clinging material emphasized her high, full breasts and slender waist; the flared hemline ended just below the knee of her long coltlike legs. She looked good and she knew it. But she felt skittish somehow, as if she were just waiting for something to happen. A quick glance at her watch confirmed the fact that it was eight o'clock as she went down for dinner.

She had one foot on the bottom step when a sound from the living room drew her to its open doorway.

"Oh, Tyler, I . . ." Carlisle stopped dead in her tracks. It wasn't Tyler but a young woman in perfectly pressed jodhpurs that came forward to meet her. There was no mistaking the hostility that flared in the dark eyes, challenging her presence. Carlisle could do no less than return the favor, wondering why the dark-haired beauty was so obviously displeased at the sight of her.

"And *who* may I ask are you?" the girl demanded, as though she had some God-given right to be there.

Carlisle was taken aback. "I beg your pardon?" she said coolly, piqued by the stranger's attitude.

The question was repeated. "I said—who are you?" The girl tossed the single thick braid of her hair over one shoulder.

"Niña, have you forgotten your manners?" Tyler Carson emerged from the kitchen at that moment, his hair still glistening from the shower.

"Tyler!" The girl raced into his arms. "I just got home and I simply had to see you!" A studied pout formed on her red lips. "But you mustn't call me a child now that I've finished school." She snuggled up to the man like some neophyte femme fatale, playfully fingering his shirt collar.

"I'll try to remember you're all grown up now." He chuckled, disentangling her arms from around his neck. "Let me introduce my guest, Maria." His voice was gently scolding, but there was a tenderness in the way he handled the girl that was new to Carlisle Scott. "This impetuous young lady is Maria Chavez, Carlisle, the daughter of one of my closest friends and neighbors. Niña, this is Miss Scott. She's here to build the new dam."

"How nice to meet you, Miss Chavez," Carlisle replied, offering her hand to the girl.

The offer was rudely ignored. "You're building a dam?" the younger woman scoffed.

Carlisle felt herself being scrutinized from the top of her dark auburn head to the tip of her handmade Italian sandals. "Yes, I am," she responded, slowly counting to ten. "I'm an engineer, you see."

"Yes, I do see." Maria sniffed disinterestedly, her attention immediately reverting to the man at her side. "Oh, Tyler, I have so much to tell you. Let's go in your study where we can be alone." She put a hand on his sleeve as she made to walk away, her impatience to have the man to herself bordering on the peevish.

"Perhaps later, Maria. Rosemary nearly has dinner ready. Would you like to stay and eat with us?" The girl visibly brightened. "Then run along to the kitchen and ask Rosemary to set a place for you."

"Yes, Tyler," she murmured.

The demure answer was entirely out of character as far as Carlisle could judge. This child was up to something and that something was doubtlessly Tyler Carson.

The man finally took a step in Carlisle's direction. "How did your first day go?"

"Better than expected . . . I think," she answered, with a tentative laugh. "All I really wanted an hour ago was a shower and a bed."

"I know the feeling," he responded with an easy camaraderie.

"That—that woman!" Maria sputtered as she shot out of the kitchen. "I'm sure I don't know why you don't fire her, Tyler. She obviously thinks she owns the place."

"Rosemary Quinn has lived one place or another on Chula Vista since before I was born, niña. She's taken care of this house and my family for nearly fifteen years. I think she has earned the right to regard this as her home, don't you?" It was a gentle, but firm put-down. Then Tyler looked past the girl to Carlisle. "I'm sure dinner is ready now. Let's go in to the dining room."

"All right," she replied, leading the way.

As the threesome settled themselves around the ornately carved dining-room table, Carlisle caught a glimpse of the sulky expression and flashing dark eyes of the young face across from her. Eyes filled with jealousy. Why, the child imagined herself to be in love with Tyler. It was all suddenly very clear to Carlisle, and it did explain, if not excuse, the girl's rudeness.

How old would Maria be? Seventeen? Perhaps eighteen? And then there was Tyler—twice the girl's age but handsome as sin. Someone Maria had no doubt looked up to all of her life. Carlisle found herself feeling rather sorry for the child. Love could be so unkind at that age.

Her speculation on the state of Maria Chavez's heart ended as Rosemary Quinn began to unveil a sumptuous meal of native foods—hot chilis, tortillas, enchiladas, and a puffy crisp bread.

"Don't know if you've had a chance to try all of these, Carlisle." The woman seemed to enjoy fussing over her. "I'll put the pitcher of iced tea right here next to you, dear. Some of them's pretty hot."

"Thank you, Rosemary."

"Hm—delicious," Tyler pronounced, taking a bite of the bread.

"It certainly is," Carlisle chimed in. "What is it?"

"Indian fry bread," supplied the man.

"It's your great-grandma's recipe, bless her soul.

Many's the time I watched her make *sopapillas*," the housekeeper said as she left them to their dinner.

Tyler turned his attention to Carlisle. "My great-grandmother came from the Taos Pueblo. She was a marvelous cook."

Carlisle felt her face grow hot, remembering how she had accused *him* of prejudice at this very table only the night before.

"His grandfather was none other than Alonso de Mendoza." Maria proudly announced this cultural tie between herself and Tyler as if it were of some special significance.

"The archaeologist?" Carlisle speculated aloud.

"The very one," Tyler confirmed. "As you see, Carlisle, I am Indian, Spanish-American, and Anglo—but above all I am a New Mexican." She felt he had neatly put her in her place.

"When are you going to take me riding, Tyler?" Maria Chavez had evidently decided she had been out of the spotlight long enough.

"We will go soon, niña, I promise," he said indulgently.

Innocent eyes were turned on Carlisle. "Do you ride, Miss Scott?"

"I assume you mean horses. I'm afraid I've only been on a horse twice in my whole life," she confessed.

The girl's expression was one of pure delight and even triumph. "How odd for someone of your age . . . although I suppose you could always *try* to learn while you're here. I'm sure Lew Hanken would have some nice tame old thing you could practice on."

"I don't imagine learning to ride a horse is much more

difficult than learning to ride a camel," Carlisle responded adroitly.

"A camel?" Maria was nonplussed.

"Yes, I learned to ride a camel rather well while I was in Egypt last year." She took a bite of enchilada before she continued. "Have you been to Egypt, Miss Chavez?"

"Tyler!" The girl turned to him for help.

Tyler Carson seemed to be thoroughly enjoying the exchange. "Never draw your claws against an expert, niña, or you may find yourself getting scratched." Then he put his head back and enjoyed a good rich laugh.

The girl's face was suffused with color. Her eyes were ablaze with malevolence as she shot a killing look. Carlisle almost wished she had not made such a point of putting the child down, even if she did deserve it. She had certainly not made a friend of Maria Chavez.

As soon as the meal concluded and an appropriate time had passed, Carlisle excused herself and escaped to her bedroom. After chain-smoking half a dozen cigarettes and reading the same page of a current best-seller several times to no avail, she finally admitted she wasn't the least bit sleepy. It was that same skittish feeling she had had earlier, rather like spring fever in June. That unaccountable restlessness that struck without warning like a virus. The only cure was to simply wait it out or . . . or take a lover. Now where had she read that? She was getting fanciful, Carlisle thought to herself, as she threw a sweater about her shoulders to ward off the evening's chill and sneaked downstairs and out the back door. A good brisk walk was just what she needed!

She had covered some distance before she turned and headed back toward the house. It was true what they said—the stars did seem brighter, the night dark and immense, out here away from the city. The sensation made her giddy, as though she had overindulged in the sangría again.

She wandered about, never straying far from the lights, until she found herself coming around the corner of the house as Maria Chavez was saying good night to Tyler. Carlisle quickly stepped back into the shadows.

"But why must that woman stay here?"

"I've explained why, Maria. Now I think that's enough about Miss Scott." The man was obviously exercising a patience he did not feel.

But the girl delivered her parting shot nevertheless. "Well, personally, I think it was really nervy showing up here bag and baggage like that."

"Carlisle is staying at Chula Vista at *my* invitation. It is no concern of yours, niña." The authority in his voice had its effect.

"I was hoping we could spend my first night back alone." She purred like a kitten, fitting herself to his side.

"Behave yourself, Maria." He laughed, giving her backside a slap.

"Ooooh—you never take me seriously!" The girl stamped her booted foot.

"If I thought you were serious, little one, I would have a talk with your father," Tyler remarked after due consideration.

Maria did not bother to disguise her excitement. "You would?"

"Yes—about sending you away to a girls' school where you couldn't get into trouble even if you wanted to."

"You wouldn't! Oh, Tyler, you do love to tease me." The girl chuckled in a low sultry voice.

"Call when you get home so I'll know you've arrived safely," he admonished, settling her into the small sports car.

So—the jodhpurs were an affectation after all, Carlisle thought.

Maria Chavez reached up then and pulled the man's head down to hers, kissing him on the cheek, but only a fraction of an inch from his mouth. "Adios," she murmured.

"Good night, Maria." Tyler stepped back as the sports car roared away into the night. He strolled toward the house, then paused and lit a small cigar and stood there a moment. "Checking up on me, Miss Scott?"

Carlisle stepped out of the shadows. "No, I wasn't sleepy, so I came out for a walk." She tilted her head and looked at the man, unknowingly issuing a challenge with her every move. "I presume that's allowed, Mr. Carson."

"What? Walking or hiding in the bushes?" He couldn't contain the grin that threatened to stretch from ear to ear. "Don't you think you're a little old for lurking about like that, Miss Scott?"

"I was not lurking about!" she indignantly refuted the charge. "It's just that I couldn't bring myself to interrupt such a tender good night." Carlisle continued, determined to wipe the grin off Tyler's face one way or another, "But don't you think she's a little young for you?"

He seemed genuinely puzzled. "Who?"

"Maria Chavez, of course."

"You've got to be kidding." He snorted.

"Not at all. The child can scarcely be more than seventeen or eighteen, while you must be"—Carlisle made a calculating circle around the man—"nearer to thirty-five yourself," she concluded.

"I am well aware of the difference in our ages and that's not what I meant. Maria is just the kid next door. A kid I've known all of her life. Hell, I'm practically old enough to be her father!"

"I know," she said pointedly.

"Now you're being ridiculous," Tyler said in an angry voice, grinding the cigar beneath his foot. "I'm not the kind of man who's interested in robbing the cradle, whatever you may think."

"There's no need to be defensive about it." She managed to instill a certain innocence into her voice. "You wouldn't be the first man swept off his feet by a pretty face. Why, I can just see it now—the lonely middle-aged cowboy and the lovely young girl next door. . . ."

Apparently Tyler had taken all he was going to take. He seized Carlisle by the arm and pulled her up against his chest, one hand holding her captive while the other went to the mass of auburn hair secured at her nape. His mouth moved deliberately only an inch or two from hers. "Actually, my dear Miss Scott, my taste in women runs more to the mature, independent type."

Carlisle snapped her head back and laughed into his face. "Does it now?"

But the laughter soon died on her lips as she became fully aware of the feel and smell of the man—the imprint of his muscular thighs through the thin material of her skirt, the faint aroma of his cigar, the lingering traces of a spicy after-shave—all mingling with the sweet scent of flowers growing nearby. It made her feel heady, even a little dizzy, being this close to him. It was downright silly! After all, Tyler Carson was a man much like other men she had known. She had no particular interest in him—or so she tried to tell herself.

Then why egg the man on knowing she was inviting his own brand of retaliation? Carlisle Scott had to be honest, if only with herself. She was curious. She wondered what Tyler's mouth would feel like on hers, the caress of his strong, calloused hands against the silky smoothness of her skin. She had felt desire rise from the strange ache inside her. She wanted to experience this man—she knew that now.

It appeared that Tyler had every intention of satisfying that curiosity, and Carlisle was suddenly nervous, unsure of herself. But before she could think any further, all thought fled with the onslaught of his lips. The man did not take hers; instead he brushed his mouth along her cheek, breathing in the scent of her. A small sound of satisfaction gurgled in the back of his throat. Then his tongue flicked around the tender shell of one ear, sending a quiver through her.

"Tyler—" She jerked her head back, only to discover the bobby pins had been removed from her normally impeccable bun. With one final tug, the swath of auburn hair cascaded over her shoulders and covered his hands. Carlisle watched in astonishment as he stuffed the handful of pins into his pants pocket.

"There—that's better," Tyler breathed, pulling her to him once more. "You did tell me you took your hair down at night. Well, it's night now."

"Yes, but . . ." Carlisle felt her face change color. Then she insinuated an outstretched palm between them. "I would like to have my bobby pins returned, please," she stated primly.

His brown eyes flickered almost humorously. "Help yourself," he challenged. But Tyler had no intention of allowing her to do so. Before Carlisle could even decide if she had the nerve to try, the assault on her senses began anew.

The man casually pushed her sweater aside to grant him access to the expanse of silky skin beneath. It clung tenuously to her shoulder for a moment before slipping unheeded to the ground. Just as she was thinking of ending the experiment, two bone-crushing hands clasped her about the rib cage as his lips burned a path along her neck and across her cheek until their mouths met at last.

His lips were surprisingly soft for a man who spent his days out-of-doors. They sipped at hers as if she were an untried vintage of sweet wine. Then—evidently convinced she was to his taste—he drank deeper and longer, his breath warming her face. Carlisle gave herself up to the experience, unaware that her hands were cupping his face as though she feared he would move away before her own thirst had been quenched.

When they finally drew apart as if by some unspoken mutual accord, the man had a knowing grin on his handsome face. "Satisfy your curiosity, Miss Scott?"

For a moment Carlisle thought of being angry with him for seeing through her so easily and then for letting her know that he had. Instead she put her head back and let out a peal of laughter, realizing her laughter was partly a defense mechanism. "No more or less than yours, cowboy," she said, equal to the occasion. "Good night, Tyler," she added quietly, undoing her hand from his.

"Carlisle . . ."

She turned back. "Yes?"

"You've forgotten your sweater." Tyler picked it up off the ground and handed it to her.

"Thank you," she mumbled politely, the words cleaving to the roof of her mouth like peanut butter.

"Anytime, ma'am," he drawled, saluting her with hand to forehead.

Carlisle swung the sweater over her shoulder and nonchalantly strolled in the front door of Chula Vista. "Anytime, ma'am!" Who did Tyler think he was kidding with that laconic cowboy act? But a neat little smile drew at the corners of her mouth as she climbed the stairs to her room.

3

~~~~~~~~~~~

The sun was a bright orange ball in a blue sky as it came up over the mountains that morning. The wind whipped across the plains with a vengeance, tossing the tall grass to and fro in its wake. It was a sight Carlisle Scott knew she would never tire of. For there was a vastness, a majesty about this "Land of Enchantment" that fired the imagination and stirred the soul.

Under her capable direction the Jeep churned along the road, spraying a cloud of dust behind it. A small whirlwind twisted and danced to one side in the gravel. Carlisle could almost discern a man's features in its midst. In her mind's eye it could only be the image of one man—Tyler Carson.

"Damn!" The vehicle shot forward as she inadvertently rammed the accelerator to the floor.

This preoccupation she seemed to have with the man

was simply going to have to stop! It had been three weeks now since their brief encounter in the moonlight and still she could not exorcise the memory of his kiss from her thoughts. It was ridiculous!

Of course, the fact that Tyler was doing an excellent job of avoiding her didn't help matters. If anything it served to magnify the events of her second night at Chula Vista out of all proportion. Carlisle had tried to figure it out and yet it remained a mystery to her, much as Tyler did himself.

She was convinced he deeply regretted that one lapse in what was otherwise strictly a business relationship. And yet there had been times, infrequent though they were, when she glimpsed some other emotion in his eyes behind a studied indifference. She tried not to think about it, but it was easier said than done during the long New Mexico nights.

She exhaled on a sigh. It didn't take a genius to recognize that Tyler was purposely working longer hours than ever. He was always gone when she came down to breakfast. It was no accident either, for she had made it a habit to arise a full hour earlier. Then, too, he was either out for dinner or took a tray to his study, where he supposedly pored over a stack of papers, or pressed some third party into service as a chaperone. Although Carlisle was sure Maria Chavez had not seen herself in that capacity the two times she had joined them. It was obvious the girl still resented her presence in Tyler's home.

But it was the man who was the enigma. Surely he did not fear she would try to make more of that one kiss than it was—simply a kiss? And yet she had never been so studiously avoided in her entire twenty-nine years. It was disconcerting to say the least.

It was irony at its finest to know that all the while Tyler was avoiding her, they were both fully aware that his bedroom was separated from hers by one small guest room. It was scarcely the Great Wall of China dividing them.

"Oh, Tyler!" The isolated laugh was followed by a break in her voice. God, she was lonely! And feeling more than a little sorry for herself as well.

Carlisle had never had trouble making friends, even in strange locations where she didn't know anyone, and if she ever found herself alone, she had been content with her own company. But now she retreated to her bedroom night after night to read or write letters or review what she wanted done on the site the next day. If the truth were told, she was tired of her own company.

Another weekend on her own held little appeal. Perhaps she would fly home to Denver on Saturday. It would of necessity be a quick trip. She would have to return Sunday evening, but she would like to see her family. Yes—she just might do that!

With her mind made up on that point, Carlisle drove over the hill and on to the construction site. She grabbed her briefcase and jumped down from the Jeep. Her long body was slim and firm in snug pants, a paramilitary shirt that hugged her breasts, field boots, and a hat pulled forward to shade her face. She was unaware of the attractive picture she made as Bill Montoya came out of one of the trailers, stifling a yawn behind his hand.

"Good morning, Carlisle. Are you early or am I late this morning?"

"Hi, Bill." She attempted cheerfulness. "Actually, I'm early. I wanted to check out a few things before we got started. We should complete the cofferdams today."

He nodded his head, dislodging a recalcitrant strand of black hair. "You've done a damned good job, Carlisle. We're right on schedule." A hand came up to brush back the stray lock. "I'll admit I had my doubts at first. I felt the cards were stacked against you. I know there are times it still isn't easy for you, but Phil and I are behind you all the way."

"Thank you, Bill. I appreciate the vote of confidence. If only Matt Delaney would come around—I just know the rest would follow. I've run into male chauvinism before, but the man seems determined to make life miserable for me."

"Give him time, Carlisle. You're twenty years younger than Matt and a woman to boot. It takes getting used to, especially for a man like that." Bill Montoya gave her a heartening smile. "Would you like a cup of coffee, boss?"

"Sounds good to me," mumbled a sleep-tousled Phil Thompson as he fell rather than stepped from the trailer door. "You are a sight for sore eyes, boss lady, and boy, are my eyes sore this morning!"

"I take it some of my crew may have overindulged last night." She laughed, picking up on the banter.

"Oh . . . please don't mention the word 'overindulge,'" groaned the architect, obviously in some misery.

"I made us a pitcher of margaritas last night—my own special recipe," Bill Montoya explained with a sheepish grin.

"That's another word I never want to hear again," Phil added with some measure of discomfiture. "Now where's that coffee I heard Bill offer?"

"Grab your cups and follow me, gentlemen. I see Sam still has the chuck wagon open for business," Carlisle chimed in. It was actually a converted camper, of course, not a real chuck wagon. But then it was frequently hinted that whatever Sam brewed in his big tin pot, it wasn't real coffee.

Yet later that day Carlisle found herself drinking another cup of Sam's brew, all the same. At least it was something to fill the hollow feeling she had. A low grumble in the pit of her stomach made her wish she had eaten lunch after all.

The sun was hot on the back of her neck as she stood a few yards from where the excavation was proceeding under her watchful eye. Then, for some reason she was at a loss to explain later, Carlisle glanced up sharply to where Matt Delaney was operating a small scraper. She watched in disbelief as the burly figure of the man seemed to slump over the wheel. The piece of machinery continued to slowly move along the grade in front of her. Still he did not straighten up.

"Dear God!" Her words were lost in the wind as she threw the coffee cup to the ground and began to run. There was but a single thought in her mind—she had to find a way to stop that damned scraper!

The adrenaline pumped into her bloodstream as she raced alongside the scraper, keeping pace with the runaway machinery until she judged the moment to be right. Her heart was pounding in her chest as she put a foot up and propelled herself into the cab.

How she managed to move the two-hundred-pound man to one side and find the brake she was never able to explain. She did recall several days later that she had once read in the newspaper about a woman who had saved a young girl from being crushed to death by lifting a five-hundred-pound stone that had fallen on the child. It had taken three husky men to move that same stone later. Evidently, there were times when ordinary people could perform extraordinary feats.

The moment Carlisle had the scraper halted, half a dozen men crowded around the cab. "Are you all right?" shouted a rather white-faced Bill Montoya.

"Yes." She nodded her head. Then her whole attention was focused on the man lying half beneath her and Carlisle barked out orders like a seasoned army sergeant. "Bill! Juan! Help me get Matt out of the cab. The rest of you get back!"

The men hurried to obey. Between the three of them they lowered the man's inert form gently to the ground.

"Dios!" Juan muttered, making the sign of the Cross.

"I-I can't find a pulse," Carlisle breathed huskily. "Has Matt ever had any history of heart trouble?" The question was asked of no one in particular and no one knew. "Well, it sure as hell looks like a heart attack to me. We've got to get his heart started!"

Knowing every second was critical, she threw off her hat and knelt beside the man. For a moment, she, too, said a quick prayer that she could remember her CPR training. Carlisle had never had to use it in the two years since she'd taken the class. First, she made sure the man's throat was clear, and then bending over him began to massage his chest. This was periodically alternated with mouth-to-mouth resuscitation. Sweat soon beaded her forehead and upper lip as she labored to revive the man.

"Frank, get on the CB and radio for an ambulance. Then get hold of Tyler. He's somewhere in the area with Doc George this afternoon. Get them here pronto!" Bill Montoya shouted to one of his men. A flurry of activity ensued, but Carlisle was all but oblivious to it. "Grab a blanket, Juan! We've got to shade them from the sun the best we can," the foreman continued to shout orders. "Does anyone else here know the emergency procedure Carlisle is using?" The blank stunned faces of his men gave Bill his answer. "Hang in there, Carlisle," came the whispered entreaty. "Help will be here any minute."

It seemed like an eternity or two passed while she fought to get Matt's heart beating. Perspiration ran down her face, her arms ached like those of a long-distance swimmer, and still she worked on. Then a hoarse moan came from the man beneath her. His eyes fluttered open for a moment and then closed again. Carlisle bit back the cry of relief that threatened to surface and waited. She felt for a pulse. It was weak, but it was there, and Matt Delaney was once more breathing on his own.

She put her face down next to the man's and spoke in a low, calm voice. "Just lie still, Matt. Don't try to speak or move. Help is on the way." She remained in a kneeling position at his side, watching for any signs that her efforts might need to be renewed. "You're going to be all right now, Matt." She gently put her hand over the one that lay at his side.

They did not have long to wait. Carlisle heard a vehicle

drive up, followed by the familiar tone of Tyler Carson's voice. Was there any sweeter sound in the whole world?

A man she presumed to be Doc George knelt by her side and took Matt Delaney's hand in his. "What happened?" he asked.

"Heart attack, I think," she whispered back.

"His pulse is weak, but there's nothing else to be done until the rescue unit arrives," he reported to Tyler in a low voice. "They'll have the equipment to stabilize his condition until we can get him to the hospital."

Carlisle remained motionless, never taking her eyes from the man's face until a pair of strong hands and a deep voice brought her to her senses.

"We'll take him now, ma'am."

She stepped back then and let the paramedics take over, her part in all of this at an end. They quickly had Matt on a stretcher, oxygen feeding into his lungs from a portable unit as they moved him into the awaiting ambulance.

"I'll go along in the ambulance," Doc George volunteered as they were preparing to leave. "Once we get Matt to the hospital, I'll give you a call at the house."

"Thanks, George," Tyler said, putting a hand on his friend's shoulder.

Carlisle finally permitted herself to exhale. "Thank God, there was a doctor nearby."

"George is a vet," Tyler corrected absently, "although he has treated the two-legged variety of animal on more than one occasion."

They all stood around for a few minutes, watching the ambulance drive away.

Then everyone seemed to shake off the paralysis of silence at once. A half-dozen voices began to speak all at the same instant.

"Tyler, you should have seen her!" Bill Montoya exclaimed. "Carlisle was the only one who realized what had happened. She ran like the wind itself. When I saw her jump up on that moving scraper my heart stopped cold."

"Never saw anything like it," added another man, shaking his head. "Hell, I just stood there in shock. The lady here was the one who did something about it."

"Matt Delaney would be a dead man right now if it weren't for the boss," Juan chimed in.

Apparently, Juan Cortez spoke for most of the men, for a chorus of similar comments came from the crowd that had gathered around Tyler and Carlisle. She suddenly realized she had unwittingly earned the respect of her crew, down to the last man. Yet she would have given anything if she could have done so through less drastic means. She felt as if she wanted to laugh and cry at the same time as a delayed reaction to the chain of events finally hit her. Her knees began to tremble in the oddest manner, and she wondered if she could manage to stay on her feet at all. Just as she buckled beneath her own weight, two strong arms came around her.

"Okay, Bill, let's wrap it up here for the day. I'll let you and the men know about Matt as soon as I hear from George. Everyone report back to work first thing tomorrow morning. I'm going to take Carlisle home now." Tyler gave his instructions as he guided her toward the Jeep.

"Right, Tyler. I'll drop your pickup off at the house this evening."

"Thanks, Bill," he called back over his shoulder.

"All right, you heard the man—let's get it wrapped up for today!" the foreman shouted to the crew.

Tyler nestled the woman's head against his shoulder. For once Carlisle was perfectly willing to have him take over. It wasn't every day that one stopped a runaway piece of machinery and very probably saved another human being's life.

"You've been a very brave girl." He stopped her with a gesture of conciliation. "I didn't mean for that to sound patronizing. It's just that you seem so pale. Do you think you can make it back to the ranch house all right?"

"Yes, but . . ."

"Sh!" The man tucked her into the passenger's seat and pulled away from the site.

Carlisle caught the tip of her tongue between her teeth and groaned with exasperation. "Oh—I've forgotten my briefcase."

"To hell with your infernal briefcase!" Tyler's lips were suddenly white with tension. "You can always get the damned thing tomorrow."

Stunned by his violent outburst, Carlisle could only stare in disbelief. For some reason she could not bear the thought of him being angry with her. Quickly she turned her head away and pretended to gaze out across the grasslands that stretched on and on around her. Hot stinging tears pricked the corners of her eyes until everything was one big blur. Her heart felt as though it were breaking into a million little pieces. But so help her

God, she wasn't going to let Tyler see how much his words had wounded her.

"Carlisle?" She could feel his eyes on her. "Carlisle!" He shot the word at her.

Then without warning, Tyler slammed on the brakes, bringing the Jeep to a full stop in the middle of the road. He firmly turned her face around to his.

"N-no . . ." She choked, trying to brush away the tears that coursed down her cheeks.

"Oh, God, honey—" the man moaned through his hands. "I didn't mean to make you cry." Tyler let out a long sigh and rested his forehead against hers. "I'm not angry with you, you know. It's—it's just when I think that you could have been killed this afternoon . . ." His voice grew softer, almost as if he were caressing her with his words. "Do you understand?"

"I-I think so." She hiccuped, not really understanding, but too confused to question him further.

"Here—you'd better dry your eyes," Tyler said, offering her his handkerchief. "Rosemary would never forgive me if she knew I had made you cry."

The remainder of the drive passed in silence, for which Carlisle was eternally grateful. She didn't feel up to talking. Not yet, anyway. She wasn't sure which event of a rather eventful afternoon had affected her more—Matt Delaney's near accident or the scene with Tyler. Either way, she was shaken more than she cared to admit. Carlisle was content now to simply put her head back against the seat and rest.

She must have dozed off, for the next thing she knew Tyler was bringing the Jeep to a screeching halt in front of the adobe ranch house. Despite her rather vocal protests, the man insisted upon carrying her into the living room where he finally deposited her on the sofa. Having heard the commotion, Rosemary Quinn came bustling in after them, worry lines creasing her normally serene features.

"Is she all right?" The query was directed at Tyler.

"Yes, she's just had a bit of a shock. There was an accident at the site—or there would have been without Carlisle's quick thinking. Apparently, Matt Delaney had a heart attack. Get a cold cloth, Rosemary. Will you please? And a good strong shot of whiskey, I think."

Tyler crouched beside the sofa and undid Carlisle's boots. He slipped them off her feet, letting them drop, mud and all, onto the carpet without a second thought. She sank back into the cushions with a sigh, content for the moment to be pampered.

"How are you feeling now?" he asked solicitously, pressing the cool cloth to her forehead and urging the whiskey down her throat. She rather liked this gentle side to his nature, a side he infrequently allowed to surface.

"I'm much better, thank you." And she truly was, though the alcohol had made her a little light-headed.

"Once you feel up to it, I'll help you to your room. I think you should get undressed and go straight to bed. We'll bring your dinnner up on a tray."

Perhaps it was the whiskey on an otherwise empty stomach that loosened her tongue, but at these words Carlisle sat up with a jerk, tossing the washcloth on the coffee table in front of her with a resounding thud. "Oh, for heaven's sake, Tyler, Matt Delaney was the one who had heart failure, not me! I'm fine. Look—I appreciate

your concern and the fact that you drove me home"—
the word slipped out unintentionally—"but I'm all right
now." She found the part of the shrinking violet one she
could play only so long before she became impatient.

"Feisty little thing, aren't you?" he responded, humor
lighting his eyes so they shone like two dark pools.

"I'm not feisty and I am most certainly not a 'little
thing.' I have *never* been little," she lectured him properly. "Why, I'll have you know, Tyler Carson, that I've been
five feet eight inches tall since the age of fourteen." It was
a bold announcement.

Tyler slowly looked her over from head to toe. "It's
funny, ma'am, but you don't seem that tall," he drawled
in his laconic cowboy voice.

"Well"—the Ls went on for some time— "I might be a
shade closer to five seven than five eight," Carlisle said,
blushing to the tips of her auburn hair. Good Lord, she
hadn't blushed in years!

Tyler leaned toward her menacingly. "Exactly how tall
are you?" His eyes pinned her to the sofa.

"Five feet seven and one-quarter inches," she confessed, in a small voice.

"I see!" It was a very dramatic "I see," as if he had
discovered some deep dark secret about her—and perhaps he had at that. Then his laugh unfurled, rich and
vibrant. He seemed to find the incident far more amusing
than Carlisle felt it was.

"Tyler!" She punctuated his name by swatting him
with a throw pillow from the sofa.

He pulled himself together with a visible effort and
adopted a serious expression. "Since you're obviously

your old self again, why don't you tell me exactly what happened this afternoon?"

Carlisle acquiesced with a shrug. "All right, but some of it is a little vague to me." She settled back to tell her story. "I was standing near the excavation, drinking a cup of Sam's coffee." That brought a wry smile to her lips. "For some reason I looked up to where Matt Delaney was running his scraper." Her hands expressed the nervous energy that still raced through her at the thought. "All of a sudden, I saw Matt slump over the wheel. When he didn't move right away I knew something was dreadfully wrong. I could feel it. It all happened in a second or two, but it was like I was watching the whole thing in slow motion. Do you know what I mean?" She glanced up for some sign that he did.

"I think so." He murmured his encouragement as he refilled her glass and helped himself to the same. "Go on."

"Well, I knew I had to stop the thing, so I took off running. The scraper wasn't moving very fast. When the moment seemed right, up I went." She shrugged her shoulders. "Bill and Juan helped me get Matt to the ground. As soon as I realized there wasn't any pulse, I started cardiopulmonary resuscitation. Thank God, Matt regained consciousness. I don't know how much longer I could have kept it up."

"You certainly kept a cool head. Few women . . . or men could have done what you did today." There was a new respect in Tyler's voice.

"I was scared to death! I'd never actually used CPR on a human being before. I even thought I might have forgotten my training. I hope Matt Delaney is going to be all right," she said, in a low fervent voice, taking a too-large gulp of her drink.

"At least he has a chance, thanks to your quick thinking."

Tyler sat down beside her on the sofa, a drink in one hand, the other coming up to encircle her neck. Carlisle could feel his hand shaking ever so slightly as he rubbed his thumb back and forth in a mesmerizing motion just below her ear. She shivered at his touch in spite of herself.

He was very quiet. Then he caught his breath; it sounded like a groan. "You could have been badly hurt or worse jumping up on a moving scraper that way."

"I guess I could have been." Carlisle tried to make light of it. "But it's hardly the kind of thing you think about at the time." Her voice seemed distant even to her own ears. She was only conscious of Tyler's touch, his nearness, and the odd effect he was having on her pulse.

"Excuse me, Tyler." Rosemary appeared at the doorway. "There's a telephone call for you. It's George Henson at the hospital."

"Thank you, Rosemary. I'll be back in a minute, honey." He put his drink down and left the room.

When Tyler returned ten minutes later, there was a broad grin on his face. Why, he looked ten years younger, Carlisle thought. He had really been worried. Beneath that mask of self-control and humor the man cared deeply. He walked straight to her, bent over, and gave her a smacking kiss full on the lips.

"Matt Delaney's all right?" She was panting, robbed of breath by his kiss.

"He's doing great! The doctor said thank God you knew what to do. It made the difference between life and death for Matt." He sat down at her side again. "Have I told you I think you're quite a woman, Carlisle Scott?"

Then he bent his head to hers once more, but this kiss was very different from the first. The first had been an outburst of joy and relief at the good news about Matt Delaney. The second carried a message, too, but it was of a far more personal nature. It began with a surprising tenderness that said he was grateful she had escaped unharmed. It went on to speak of desire and need and want.

Carlisle knew now that the first unforgettable kiss of three weeks ago had been in the back of Tyler's mind as well. She felt herself moving toward him, melting into his bones as she eagerly opened her mouth beneath his. She wanted to be a part of his strength, of his very body. Tyler drank from her sweetness as though he wanted to consume her, to take her inside of him.

His hand slipped down her arm until it was level with her breast. His fingers reached out and found the hard button beneath her shirt that was unmistakable evidence of her arousal. She could feel the heat of his hand through the material, imprinting her flesh with his brand.

What was it about one man's kiss, one man's touch, that could thrill a woman to the very core of her being, while all the others left her cold? Was this love or only that strange animal called passion? Whatever it was, it happened for Carlisle Scott then and there. She felt herself opening to Tyler as a flower opens to the sunrise. She held nothing back from him, meeting his desire and need with her own.

When they finally moved apart, Carlisle was trembling within as well as without. "I should save someone more often," she murmured, in a husky voice.

"Can I be next?" Tyler formed the question against the soft tumble of hair that had come undone in the fracas. He held her loosely in his embrace, reluctant to have her leave his arms. "If I don't stop kissing you right now, woman, Rosemary could get the shock of her life the next time she ventures into this room." There was something in his tone that warned her he was only partially teasing her.

It was a warning she chose to ignore. "And we wouldn't want to shock poor Rosemary, now would we?" The gleam in her eye dared him to do otherwise.

"Don't ever dare a 'middle-aged' cowboy, honey." The reference to his age was one she had once thrown in his face earlier. "You could get more than you'd bargained for."

"Oh, I don't know about that . . ."

He firmly put her away from him. "Well, I do! I'm going to call Bill with the good news about Matt. I think it would be an excellent idea if you went upstairs and lay down for a couple of hours."

"I might do that." Her voice floated through the air like a disembodied spirit. "I'm feeling terribly sleepy." Carlisle yawned right on cue, as if to substantiate her claim.

They proceeded to part company at the foot of the stairs—Tyler in the direction of his study and Carlisle to her room. In atypical fashion, she discarded her clothing piece by piece as she weaved toward the bed. She climbed between the sheets attired only in a lacy bra and a pair of panties. She was still softly humming to herself when she drifted off to sleep.

She may have drifted off to sleep, but she certainly did not return from dreamland the same way. Carlisle awoke with a start as the bedroom door swung open and an emphatically male voice called out to her.

"Time to wake up, sleepyhead! Your dinner is here."

"Go away!"

"Carlisle—"

"You're not Rosemary." A groggy brain made her state the accusation aloud as she struggled to an upright position.

Tyler gave her one of his boyish grins. "You noticed . . ."

Carlisle self-consciously tugged the sheet up under her arms as she found Tyler studying her bare skin. He placed the tray on her lap and retreated only a matter of inches to sprawl across the end of her bed.

She unfolded the napkin and took the fork in her hand before she permitted herself to speak. "Are you going to sit there and watch me eat?"

Tyler shrugged as if the matter were out of his hands. "Rosemary's orders—and I always do what Rosemary tells me." He grinned wolfishly.

"Aren't you hungry?" she asked as she delved into the western omelet with unconcealed relish. It had been a good fourteen hours since she had last eaten.

"Yes—but I've had my dinner already." His expression told her that food was *not* what he had on his mind.

Carlisle took another bite of omelet, but between balancing the tray on her lap, fighting to keep the sheet in place, and eating, it missed her mouth and neatly dropped into the hollow between her breasts. In the process, the sheet slipped down around her waist, leaving far more of her exposed than she cared to think.

"Tyler!" It was a cry for help.

The man took a tissue from the box on the bedside table and gallantly plucked the offending bit of omelet from its landing place.

Her eyes flashed green with indignation. "That's not what I meant!"

"I was only trying to help, Carly," he said without a trace of emotion.

"Sure you were—" she said skeptically.

"Wait a minute—I have the perfect solution." Tyler propelled himself off the bed and out the door before she could utter one word of inquiry. He returned several minutes later with a white T-shirt tucked under his arm. Carlisle watched transfixed as he removed the tray from her lap and stated in a fatherly voice, "Arms up!"

He slipped the shirt over her head and fussed with its arrangement, until she was forced to slap his hand like a parent scolding a naughty child.

"Have you quite finished, Mr. Carson?"

"I haven't even begun, *Miss* Scott."

"If you're going to insist on playing games, then I wish you would do it elsewhere." She sniffed, trying to recover her composure.

"I promise to behave myself—for now." Tyler returned to his former posture at the foot of the bed. "By the way, we've been invited to a party at the Chavez ranch tomorrow evening. With all the excitement I haven't had a chance to tell you."

"But . . ."

"No, 'buts,' Carlisle. We either go together or not at all." He was adamant.

"Say what you will, I'm quite sure the Chavezes have no interest in including me in their party. I know Maria won't want me there." She wasn't asking for sympathy, simply stating the truth as she saw it.

"I want you there." He emphasized each word.

Carlisle put a hand to her head. "You're making this very difficult for me, Tyler."

"Do you have a headache, honey?"

She jerked her head up. "I *never* have headaches."

His brown eyes flashed with good old-fashioned mirth. "Good, I'll keep that in mind. It's settled then. Be ready about eight o'clock tomorrow evening. Now you'd better eat your dinner or Rosemary will give me what for."

"Someone should have given you what for a long time ago," Carlisle muttered under her breath as she took another bite of her dinner.

4

No! No! No!"

Carlisle tore the dress off and threw it down on the bed. It fell in a crumpled heap, joining the evening's other rejects. Why she had ever bought the damned thing in the first place was beyond her. She looked lousy in pink.

She puffed out her cheeks, bright red from exertion, and let out an exasperated hiss—a vocal expression of her frustration. She glanced up and caught sight of herself in the full-length mirror on the closet door.

Carlisle studied her body with a critical eye. She saw a tall lithe figure with slightly tanned skin, full perky breasts, and long shapely legs which she personally considered her best feature. A riot of auburn hair tumbled around her bare shoulders, a few wispy strands floating about the flushed cheeks. Impulsively, impishly she stuck out a pink tongue at her reflection and went back to the business of finding something to wear.

"Yes, I think this will do," she murmured, holding up yet another outfit. Her final choice was a dusky rose sundress with thin spaghetti straps that shimmered in the same shade as her hair. She loosely tied an oversized kerchief of the same diaphanous material about her bare shoulders.

Carlisle slipped her feet into skimpy high-heeled sandals, added a slim gold chain to her wrist and gold hoops to her ears. Her only bow to local flavor was a Spanish comb with which she secured her hair at the nape of her neck. She had decided from the start not to wear anything that had the slightest appearance of putting her in competition with the lovely dark-haired, dark-eyed Maria, although there was a beautiful Spanish-style dress in her closet.

Her choice finally made, Carlisle's innate sense of orderliness returned. She tidied the bedroom with quick efficient movements, neatly hanging the discarded garments back in her closet. She marveled at her own indecisiveness. It was so unlike her.

She had put the finishing touches to her makeup and picked up an embroidered drawstring evening bag when one clipped knock sounded on the bedroom door.

"Yes?" she called out, turning around as Tyler came into the room.

He was impeccably dressed in a semi-western style suit of burnished brown that brought out the bronze highlights of his thick brown hair. She eyed the tooled boots with admiration, the soft feltlike Stetson with a silvered band that he held in his hand. Unlike the popularized version of western attire, his was genuine and had no doubt long been the style in this part of the country.

"You look lovely," he pronounced at last.

"Thank you. You're rather stunning tonight yourself," she mused, the corners of her mouth turning up into a smile.

"I confess I found your chinos attractive, but *this* is no less than a transformation. You're a beautiful woman, Carlisle." The deep baritone was relaxed and easy, but the woman could feel his eyes boring into her.

She executed a small curtsy. "Thank you again, kind sir."

Tyler advanced one step. "Perhaps we *should* skip this party. . . ."

"Oh, no you don't, Tyler Carson!" she remonstrated, all the while knowing he couldn't possibly mean it. "Not after I've tried on every damned dress in my closet!"

"You're not—nervous, are you?" He hesitated as he spoke.

"Perhaps just a little," she answered him truthfully. "You and Maria are the only two people I'll know, and I scarcely think she will welcome me with open arms."

"Maria is just a kid. Don't let her bother you. Believe me, everyone is going to adore you." Tyler stood to one side and indicated the open doorway with a sweep of his hat. "If you're ready, Miss Scott . . ."

The night air was fresh and fragrant, though a cross breeze occasionally wafted the unmistakable aroma of livestock to her nostrils. Carlisle involuntarily wrinkled up her nose. She supposed it simply took getting used to, much as the noise and fumes of the city might to someone from the wide-open spaces.

"It's not fancy or fine, but it's all mine." Tyler laughed as he escorted her to the awaiting pickup truck. "I did have some of the boys spruce it up a bit this afternoon, ma'am. I hope it meets with your approval."

"I'm sure it will," Carlisle replied, as if she were puzzled by something he'd said. "Tyler—are you always in such a good mood or did you get a head start on this party tonight?"

"Are you referring to alcohol, ma'am? Rest assured, the stuff never touches my lips."

She looked at him askance. She had seen Tyler angry, cool as a cucumber, passionate, and even tender, but the quality she most marveled at was his unrelenting sense of humor, corny though it was at times.

"Actually, I think it comes from living alone for so long. You get kind of crazy with no one to talk to night after night." It was undoubtedly the most revealing statement he had ever made to her about himself.

"Why haven't you married then?" It seemed the natural question to ask.

The man neatly turned the tables on her. "Why haven't you?"

"I've considered it several times, but few men want to be married to a professional unless she more or less gives up that profession. I couldn't do that."

"Not even for love?" he asked casually.

"Not even for love. A woman doesn't ask a man to give up everything for marriage. I don't know why men expect it of women."

"Hm . . ." He seemed to consider this for a moment.

"But you never said why you haven't married." Carlisle studied him, head cocked.

Tyler gave it about thirty seconds of thought before answering. "Finding a woman with a mind as well as a body isn't easy when you live in a remote area like this and work twelve to fourteen hours a day running a ranch. It isn't an easy life, Carlisle. You don't rush into it without a lot of thought."

"Perhaps you've never been in love, Tyler?" An indiscreet question perhaps and one that could easily bring a host of denials and lies to his lips, but Carlisle prayed he would be truthful with her just this once. She could feel his tenseness across the space that separated them.

"I was in love once. It was a long time ago."

"What went wrong?" she asked with nonchalance, for she was certain something *had* gone wrong.

"She decided she couldn't spend the rest of her life buried in a remote ranch in New Mexico." Carlisle could detect no pain in Tyler's voice, no residue of bitterness.

"She wasn't from this area?"

"No, she wasn't from around here," he said in a conversational tone. "I met her back East."

"Back East? I didn't realize . . ." She paused, indecisive.

"I left New Mexico when I was eighteen," he said by way of explanation. "I spent four years studying animal husbandry at Penn State and then enlisted in the Peace Corps. I was going to change the world in those days." He sounded tired. "I came back to the States two years later, much older and wiser, and enrolled in law school at

George Washington University. That's where I met Alicia. We fell in love and got engaged. I was sure I had it all right there in the palm of my hand," he murmured, almost to himself.

"You never told me," she said softly, stunned by this insight into a man she suddenly realized she knew so little of.

"No, I guess not," he replied. "I stayed away a long time, Carlisle. Too long. My father wasn't getting any younger, and running the ranch became too much for him. He had a severe stroke one day and died the next." Now there was pain in his voice.

"Oh, Tyler, I'm sorry." It was inadequate, but what could she say?

"After Dad died, I came home, of course. I intended to stay just long enough to settle his business and then return to school, to the life I had made for myself. But it was the funniest thing—I discovered that this was where I wanted to be. This was my future. Unfortunately Alicia couldn't see it as hers, so we agreed to break off the engagement. I've been running the ranch ever since." He stated the facts with few regrets for the road he had taken.

"How long has that been?" Carlisle admitted to curiosity.

"Nearly nine years now."

"But all that time, Tyler—haven't you thought of marrying?"

"Sure I have," he scoffed at her naïveté, "but like I said earlier, finding the right woman isn't something I've had a lot of time to do."

There was something in his voice that drifted to her

77

through the darkness, but she couldn't quite put her finger on it.

"What about you?" There was the slightest hesitancy in his tone. "Have you been in love with many men?"

It was her turn to scoff. "I don't think the history of my affairs of the heart could possibly be of any interest to you."

Tyler uttered an impatient noise. "Don't be coy, Carlisle, not after I've just bared my soul to you."

"I would hardly call what you did 'baring your soul,'" she said, offhandedly, knowing there was far more he had left unsaid.

"Perhaps not, but it's more than I've told anyone in a long time."

"I-I'm sorry, Tyler," she began, then swallowed roughly. "I thought I was in love a couple of times," she admitted, since this was evidently a night for confessions. "The first man wanted me to stay home and be a conventional housewife. I couldn't do that." Carlisle paused to put out her cigarette and to instill indifference into her voice. It was much more difficult for her to speak of Wade even after two years. "The second man was perfectly willing for me to continue with my career and even the travel involved, as long as I didn't question his activities while I was away. I wasn't cut out for that kind of 'open marriage' and told him so. That ended our relationship."

Carlisle failed to mention the rumors she had heard later. Rumors that Wade had been seeing someone else the entire time he had supposedly been in love with her.

"He hurt you badly." The disembodied voice commented softly.

"I got over it." Yes, she had gotten over Wade, but not without a lot of tears and sleepless nights. Carlisle knew she had been a little disillusioned about men ever since.

"We're a fine pair, aren't we, Carlisle Scott?" Tyler's voice carried a heavy layer of sarcasm. "But it's all ancient history now."

"Yes—it's ancient history now," she repeated.

She gestured blindly in his direction without looking at him, unaware that she sounded disinterested. It wasn't true, of course. She *was* interested, terribly so, but she was also trying to decipher whether there was a message for her in what he had said. "It's a lovely night, isn't it?" she finally ventured.

When that elicited no response, she sat back and tried to enjoy the drive to Hacienda del Sol. She was amazed by the distance they had to travel just to reach the neighboring ranch. Everything about this country was larger than life. It was as if a bolder hand had created the shadowy mountains and sea of grass on either side of the road.

Carlisle took a deep steadying breath as Tyler drove up in front of the white stucco hacienda. He quickly found a place to park in a grove of trees.

Hacienda del Sol had the traditional terra-cotta roof and arched porticos with wrought-iron gates that characterized Spanish architecture. Upon entering the courtyard, they beheld a magnificent circular fountain and beyond two oversized and ornately carved doors.

"Why, it's fantastic! Why didn't you tell me?" she murmured as they approached the entrance.

He merely smiled and shrugged. "There are a number of things I've been meaning to talk to you about, Carlisle—but quite honestly, architecture wasn't one of them."

She opened her mouth and then closed it without speaking. Her attention was drawn to the smiling couple who came forward to greet them. "It was very kind of you to invite me this evening, Señora and Señor Chavez. Your home is beautiful," she extolled.

"Thank you, Miss Scott. It is a pleasure to finally meet you. But please, I am Simonita to my friends and I will call you Carlisle," the gracious black-haired woman insisted, her mature beauty an indication of what Maria might one day be.

"And I am Ramón," stated the handsome man at Simonita's side. "We have heard of your exploits at the dam site, Miss Scott. I must say you are as beautiful as you are brave." The gentleman—and there was no other word that more aptly described Ramón Chavez—simply oozed charm and old-world grace that Carlisle found enchanting.

"Thank you," she murmured prettily, feeling herself flush with pleasure at his words.

"*Qué fiesta más agradable*, Simonita! What a lovely party!" Tyler exclaimed to his hostess.

"*Gracias*, Tyler." The woman smiled. "And how is your dear mother these days?"

"She's well, Simonita. Life in Phoenix agrees with her."

"You must show Carlisle about while we greet our other guests." The woman swept one hand through the air as if to caress Carlisle's cheek. *"Es una chica encantadora!"*

"She said you're charming," Tyler translated, as he grasped Carlisle by the elbow and steered her into the large front hall.

The Chavez home was a showplace of beautiful things—dark, richly carved furnishings, tiled floors with handwoven rugs, intricate wall hangings of hammered brass and silver, paintings by well-known artists like Peter Hurd and Georgia O'Keefe. There was a round, half-moon fireplace in the main room and an ornate pair of hammered birds ensconced overhead, a thick candle between their claws. Carlisle tried not to stare at the sumptuous buffet in the dining room, where she caught a glimpse of a crystal teardrop chandelier, several primitive paintings, and a beautiful écru lace tablecloth on the pedestal-legged table.

The throbbing sounds of a Spanish guitar emanated from the patio off the living room. A handsome young man was perched atop a high stool with a beautiful guitar in his hands. Lanterns lit the path that wound through the walled garden behind him.

It was the most romantic setting Carlisle thought she had ever seen. She felt as if she had somehow been transported to another time and another place. A shiver ran through her as the music touched some responding chord within her. No translation was needed to understand the plaintive song of love and love lost.

"Sometimes it is enough to simply *feel*," Tyler said, as if reading her mind.

"Good evening, Miss Scott." The moment of intimacy

was shattered as they were approached by a man whose face was somehow familiar. "We've never been properly introduced, but I'm George Henson." He took her hand in his. He didn't shake it or kiss it, but simply held it for a moment.

"The veterinarian." She smiled. "I was very happy to see you yesterday." Carlisle cranked her neck back to look up at the man. George Henson must have been three or four inches over six feet tall, with loose shoulders and a teenage lankiness that defied the twenty years that had passed since he had indeed been a teenager.

"And I'm very happy to see you tonight. We've been wondering when Tyler would let the rest of us meet you." His eyes were riveted to the bewitching face before him.

"Good evening, George." A somewhat gruff voice sounded at her side. She noticed Tyler still had her rather possessively by the arm.

"Hello, Tyler." The two men exchanged handshakes. The tension Carlisle had sensed for just a moment seemed to have passed.

Then the whirlwind of introductions and names began. Carlisle was overwhelmed by the down-to-earth friendliness of everyone she met. Several of the younger men did try to woo her from Tyler's side, but he skillfully managed to ward them off with a word or a look. She found herself amused rather than offended by his unmistakable attitude of hands off.

In the next hour, Carlisle was quite sure she met every single person at the party, with Tyler at her side, of course. They were talking to another rancher and his wife when Simonita Chavez appeared discreetly on the perimeter of the group. Her face was taut with lines of distress she was obviously trying to conceal with no small effort. Without interrupting the conversation, their hostess neatly cut Tyler from the pack. As the twosome moved away Carlisle felt her ears perk up at the mention of Maria's name.

"I-I'm sorry, Carol. What did you say?" She turned back to the woman who was speaking.

"I know you're working awfully hard, Carlisle, but Mike and I would be delighted if you and Tyler could join us for dinner one evening. Say next Friday?" The pretty brunette posed with a smile.

"We'd love to!" Then Carlisle caught herself. "I'll have to ask Tyler first, of course."

Carol Martin shook her head from side to side. "Poor Simonita—she and Ramón have their hands full with that Maria, I'll tell you. I suppose it's always more difficult with the youngest child, especially when it's a girl. I'd say Maria has surely led her parents a merry chase."

"Now, Carol . . ." Mike put a restraining hand on his wife's arm.

"Well, Carlisle is bound to hear things, Mike. Everyone knows that the girl makes a regular pest of herself over at Chula Vista. Tyler's just too nice a man to tell her to bug off." Carol giggled at her own pun, unintended though it had been.

"I'm sure Tyler can handle Maria Chavez without your help, my dear. Let's face it—what man in his right mind would pay any attention to a kid of seventeen when someone like Miss Scott is right there under his roof?" The man flushed red. "No offense intended, Carlisle," he quickly added in a sober voice.

"No offense taken, Mike," she just as quickly assured

him. "Everyone seems determined to pair me off with Tyler, but our relationship is strictly business, you know."

"Well, I for one couldn't be more pleased to hear that," remarked George Henson, as he joined them. "Since it does appear that Tyler is otherwise engaged, may I escort you to the buffet, Carlisle?"

Determined to put any rumors to rest, she hooked her arm through his and smiled up at the man. "I'd be delighted, George. You'll have to promise to help me now," she went on as they made their way into the dining room, "some of these dishes are a real mystery to me."

The veterinarian cleared his throat and handed her a plate. "We'll start with some nachos—those are strips of fried tortilla, cheese, and hot green peppers. Here, try one," he said, popping the spicy hot canapé into her mouth.

"Simply delicious," she replied hoarsely, adding another to her plate.

"This may be more to your taste." The man laughed. "It's *arroz con pollo*—chicken with rice and vegetables. "It's nonchilied and not in the least bit hot."

Carlisle nodded and thankfully helped herself to some of the dish, then to some lightly fried loops sprinkled with confectioners' sugar that she knew to be Spanish fritter crisps. At the end of the table was a tray of sliced melon—honeydew, cantaloupe, and watermelon garnished with quarters of fresh limes, sticks of fresh pineapple, fresh raspberries. Two silver shakers, one filled with cinnamon, one with powdered ginger, were placed nearby. They concluded with several spiced nuts each.

"It looks delicious, George, but do you really think we're going to be able to eat all of it?" Carlisle laughed as she followed him to a cozy table set for two out on the patio. She had noticed perhaps a dozen similar arrangements placed about the house and patio.

"Sure we will, and when we're finished I'll get us some Spanish coffee."

"Spanish coffee? Sounds intriguing."

"It's coffee and hot chocolate mixed in equal amounts. Simonita always serves it with a stick of cinnamon and a topping of thick cream." He smacked his lips expressively.

"I'm going to gain ten pounds and feel terribly fat if I eat like this the entire three months I'm here." Carlisle groaned.

"As a doctor, I can assure you there's nothing wrong with your figure, Miss Scott."

"Enjoying yourself, George?" Tyler magically appeared between them, the deep furrow of a scowl plowing across his forehead.

"Oh—hello, Tyler. Care to join us?" George blithely extended the invitation.

"Yes, I would." He plunked his plate down on the table as he pulled up an extra chair.

"Have you had a chance to see any of the sights yet?" The veterinarian addressed the question to Carlisle as though they had never been interrupted.

"Not yet, but I intend to," she replied, jerking her attention from Tyler's face.

"You really should visit Taos and the Pueblo while you're here and E-town might be of special interest to you as an engineer."

"What's E-town?" Carlisle's curiosity was aroused.

"Elizabethtown is an old ghost town up in the Sangre

de Cristo mountains. It has a water system you might find interesting. I would be glad to drive you up that way if you're not busy one day."

Tyler cut in, his voice razor sharp. "Thanks for the offer, George, but I'll show Carlisle anything she wants to see."

She could almost feel the other man carefully back off. "Sure, Tyler."

Carlisle got to her feet. "Well, if you two gentlemen will excuse me, I think I'll go powder my nose."

"It's up the stairs and the first door on your right." Tyler supplied the answer before she even asked the question.

"Thank you," she said stiffly and heaved a rather big sigh of relief as she made her way to the second-floor bathroom. She didn't know what Tyler had to be irked about, anyway. He was the one who had left her. Besides, George Henson was fun.

Carlisle quickly freshened her makeup and gave an unnecessary brushing to her hair before stepping back out into the hallway.

"Well—if it isn't our Miss Scott!" A soft female voice spoke combatantly.

Carlisle put a tight rein on her temper and responded evenly. "Hello, Maria."

The girl threw her loose dark hair back from her shoulders. "Having fun, Miss Scott?"

"Yes. Yes, I am. Your parents have made me feel very welcome," she said with conviction.

"You seem to be getting pretty chummy with our local vet." Maria smiled mechanically.

"I hardly think that's any of your business."

The younger woman gave a short laugh. "Oh, I'm not complaining and I'm sure Tyler isn't either. You've been enough of an imposition on him already. The poor man shouldn't have to spend the entire evening entertaining you as well." Maria lifted her chin, a look of pure fury in her eyes. "You do know Tyler doesn't want you at Chula Vista?"

"You seem to forget I'm at Chula Vista at Tyler's invitation," Carlisle stated, her voice level.

"Well, he hardly had any choice in the matter, now did he?" The girl spoke with ill-concealed sarcasm. "You must realize that people are beginning to talk."

"Talk?" Carlisle could have kicked herself for taking the bait.

"Yes, about the two of you being alone together in his house." Maria's dark, liquid eyes were full of pleasurable malice.

"We're hardly alone," she returned calmly. "Rosemary Quinn is always there, as you well know. And I suspect the only person talking about it is you, Maria." Carlisle spun on her heel and made to walk away.

"I don't think you fully understand the situation," the girl continued, undaunted. "There's always been an—an understanding between Tyler and me that once I was old enough I would become the mistress of Chula Vista."

The woman turned and faced her opponent. "Apparently you're the only one aware of this 'understanding,' Miss Chavez. I assure you, Tyler knows nothing about it."

"Tyler Carson is mine! He belongs to me!" The girl spit the words out savagely.

Carlisle threw her head back and laughed as she said, "You don't *own* a man, especially one like Tyler Carson.

If you were a woman you would understand that. But then that's the whole point, isn't it, Miss Chavez? You're still a child, not a woman. Now if you will excuse me—Tyler is waiting." She continued down the stairs, her legs rather wobbly for all her brave talk.

Yet she did not return to the table where she had left Tyler and George Henson. Instead she sought out a quiet secluded bench in a far corner of the garden. She suddenly, inexplicably, wanted to be alone. She sat down and lit a cigarette, hoping to calm her rather shattered nerves.

Who could have foreseen that what had seemed like just another job would turn out to embroil her in a triangle with a passionate teenager and a man she found herself strongly attracted to? Damn! It was just the kind of messy emotional situation she had always tried her utmost to avoid. It would have been better for everyone involved if she had followed her first instinct and not come to this party.

Carlisle was so lost in her own thoughts, she could not pinpoint the moment the band began to play in some other part of Hacienda del Sol. But the sweet haunting music floated across the night and finally reached her ears nonetheless. The soaring melody carried by the lone violin tugged at her, enhancing the feeling of melancholy that threatened to overcome her. She squeezed her eyes shut, the breath shuddering in her lungs.

"Carlisle?" A deep male voice vibrated nearby. She opened her eyes and stared straight ahead. "What in the hell are you doing out here all by yourself?" Tyler demanded, as he forced her to make room for him beside her on the bench. "I've been looking for you everywhere."

"I . . . ah, I wanted to be alone, that's all," she said, without enthusiasm.

"Is something wrong?" he asked, with genuine concern.

"No, nothing's wrong," she replied, permitting herself a small sigh.

"Then dance with me," he said, in a low voice, pulling her to her feet. His look and voice hypnotized her to his will.

Tyler stood and opened his arms. Carlisle felt herself willingly step into the circle of his embrace. He gathered her body to him, his breath stirring the hair about her face, his lips softly nuzzling the side of her neck.

Then he drew back and gazed into her eyes. "I've wanted to hold you like this all evening." His voice was husky. In the privacy of the shadows, he took both of her arms and entwined them around his neck, his own encircled about her waist.

There was no obstacle between them now to prevent the growing awareness they had of each other. His hard muscular thigh drove into hers; her breasts were crushed to his chest. She could feel the outline of each button of his shirt pressing into her skin. Her breathing became shallow in the warm night air.

The music paused for a minute and then began anew, but the man and woman stayed in each other's arms. Everything else, everyone else, was forgotten as they swayed in perfect unison, content in their own little world. Entranced and beguiled beyond her wildest dreams, Carlisle ran her tongue along the line of Tyler's jaw, wanting to know even the taste of the man. Then she pressed a light kiss to the corner of his mouth.

"You picked one hell of a time to do that!" he growled in an agonized voice. "Don't you know I've wanted you so badly the past three weeks I've worked myself into exhaustion to keep from breaking down your bedroom door?"

Carlisle could only shake her head. "I-I didn't know. You—you seemed to go out of your way to avoid me."

"I had to, dammit! I didn't know if I could keep my hands off you!" He swore again under his breath.

Impatient now, his mouth covered hers in a kiss that told her of desire and need too long suppressed beneath a façade of indifference. Tyler's tongue tore into the soft sanctuary of her mouth; his hands molded her hips to the hard outline of his body. Carlisle felt herself consumed by his passion and yet made to feel more alive than she had ever been in her entire life. She tried to open her lips even further, drawing his breath into her own body, wanting anything that was a part of this man.

They were both visibly shaken when the kiss came to an end. She let her head rest on his shoulder, allowing him to absorb the weight of her body.

Then she happened to glance over the man's shoulder, only to encounter the flushed and glaring face of Maria Chavez, who stood watching them dance. Carlisle saw the girl turn and maliciously whisper to the woman next to her. Then they both looked up to where she and Tyler still moved in an embrace.

Carlisle couldn't take it any longer. She took the

initiative and swung Tyler around in a half circle so that her back was to Maria.

"Now you're trying to lead, too," he teased, his eyes still glazed with passion.

She inhaled a slow, trembling breath. "Look, Tyler—perhaps it would be best if I moved out of Chula Vista." The thought of wagging tongues did not bother her, but after all, these people were Tyler's friends and neighbors. She wished him no harm.

"What suddenly brought this on?" he demanded somberly. "I thought we decided weeks ago that it was the only practical course?"

"I-I just think it might be for the best—for both of us," she stammered.

She watched as his features tightened and grew dark with anger. "Are you afraid I might try to take advantage of the situation?"

"Good heavens, no." She laughed brittlely. "I'm a big girl now. I can take care of myself, in whatever way I should choose to."

He seemed satisfied it was so, then it was his turn to look beyond her shoulder. "Has Maria said something to you?"

Carlisle did not answer, but the slight, involuntary stiffening of her body told him.

"It was Maria, wasn't it?" He did not wait for her to answer—he knew. "She's been making mischief for us since the day you arrived here. I'm going to have a talk with that young woman right now!" Tyler started to pull away, anger governing his every move.

"No, Tyler, listen! It's not worth getting upset about.

I'm sure you don't want to cause a scene," she said, trying to sound reasonable. "Maria would just deny it, anyway, and this is her parents' home. If you make a fuss now, everyone will believe it's true."

He paused and then turned back to face her, his first irrational burst of anger gone. "And exactly what did little Miss Chavez say to you?"

Under his scrutiny, Carlisle felt the color rise in her face. "She said that people were beginning to talk about us being alone in your house."

"But we're not alone—Rosemary lives there, too, and they all know that," he said scornfully.

"That's what I said." She sighed, having no intention of repeating the rest of her conversation with the girl.

Tyler held up his hands, examining the palms, then lowered them to his side in a gesture of futility. "Does it bother you?" he said indistinctly.

She reached out and lightly touched his arm. "Not for myself, but these people are your friends."

"Friends? Friends don't gossip or poke their noses into things that are none of their damned business!" he hissed. "It appears that we're damned whether we've slept together or not!"

"I-I'm sorry, Tyler—truly, I am. It's my fault. I should have realized that something like this might happen. I wouldn't do anything to purposely hurt or embarrass you. I want you to know that." She couldn't prevent the tears that formed on the edges of her eyes.

"You silly adorable goose," he said softly. "I don't give a hoot what they say about me. It's you I'm worried about."

"I don't matter."

Tyler gently took her face in his hands. "You do to me, Carlisle. Haven't you guessed by now how I feel about you?" He rubbed his chin against hers in a caress that was curiously comforting.

She could only shake her head, half-afraid to guess at his meaning.

He raised his head and looked her straight in the eyes. "I think I've fallen in love with you. No, wait, there's more!" he said, cold-bloodedly. "I was angry, not only at Maria for her lousy insinuations, but at myself because I wish they were true. I have to fight like hell to keep my hands off you. I lie in my bed at night and fantasize about how it would be with you—knowing you're only a few feet away. . . ." Tyler watched the conflicting emotions cross her face. Perhaps he had said too much, too fast. But he wasn't to be stopped. "I want you, make no mistake about that. In my heart, I'm guilty of everything these people are only guessing at!" He swore under his breath, pulling her back into the lights and noise of the festive party. "No more dancing in the moonlight for you, Miss Scott, or by God, I'll really give the gossips something to talk about."

"If you don't let go of my arm, you will, anyway," Carlisle said breathlessly, unable to comprehend everything that had just been said.

He dropped her arm and pasted a ridiculously nonchalant smile on his handsome face. "You're right, of course."

She felt the laughter bubble up inside her until it surfaced on her lips. "Oh, Tyler—you'd never make it as an actor," she said, then the laughter died away and wide hazel eyes gazed up at him solemnly. "Tyler . . . I—"

He raised an expressive brow and cut her off before she could continue. "This is supposed to be a party, so let's have some fun!"

"All right," she agreed, knowing that that moment in time—her moment—to tell him of her fears and confusion had slipped away just as quickly as it had come. Resignedly Carlisle hooked her arm through Tyler's and put on her best party face as they strolled back into the house.

5

~oooooooooooo~

The drive back to Chula Vista was a curiously silent one. It wasn't a comfortable or companionable silence, but rather a strained awareness that drew Tyler and Carlisle together even as they tried desperately to move apart.

Tyler parked the pickup in front of the ranch house and unceremoniously killed the engine. "We're home," he said cryptically, and got out of the truck.

Their entrance was effected in the same conspiracy of silence, but this time so as not to disturb the sleeping Rosemary Quinn.

"I think it would be best if we said good night down here," he stated, pitching his voice low.

"All right—good night, then," Carlisle mimicked his whisper.

"Good night," Tyler returned, then swung on his heel

and disappeared into the study. The door closed with a resounding finality.

Carlisle Scott watched the man walk away, her heart plummeting to her feet. She wanted to call him back, knowing it would take only one word from her to do so, yet she found herself incapable of uttering that one solitary word. She had thought—well, never mind what she had thought—this evening was not ending the way she imagined it would.

She wearily climbed the stairs to her bedroom on the second floor, dropped her evening bag on the dresser, and carelessly sank into a nearby chair.

It had been a rather wonderful evening, aside from the encounter with Maria Chavez. She had enjoyed meeting Tyler's friends and Tyler—a flood of emotions raced through Carlisle at the very thought of the man. She had thrilled to his touch as they danced there in the garden and when he confessed that he was falling in love with her, she had feared her heart would simply stop beating. Yet he had been so distant, so quiet on the way home. Perhaps he realized they were too different kinds of people. He represented everything she had tried to avoid in her past relationships.

Carlisle mechanically rose from the chair and began to undress. She slipped into a pair of shorty pajamas and a robe and put out the lights. Opening one of the two french doors that led out to the terrace, she stretched out on top of the bed.

There in the darkness thoughts of Tyler could no longer be held at bay. She knew she was physically attracted to the man. The gnawing ache in every bone of her body was not to be denied. But was she in love with him as well? She had thought herself in love twice before in her life. Indeed, she might have married either man if the circumstances had been different.

Carlisle had learned early that most men were intimidated by an attractive woman who was also intelligent. She had been at the top of her class in college and had proudly graduated Phi Beta Kappa. Then, with a Master's Degree in civil engineering, she had joined her father's firm. She had assumed that one day she would find a man who loved her, a man who was not threatened by her accomplishments. Now at the age of twenty-nine she was no longer certain there was a knight on a white charger out there for her. For the past several years she had tried to tell herself there would be no regrets if she chose to remain single.

But she was no longer sure of that. This man of strong passions, tenderness, and intelligence had revealed what had been missing in her life. She thought of the need he could arouse in her at his touch, and she trembled.

She felt so alive in his arms. The words of every love song she had ever heard suddenly had meaning for her. Damn! She was not immune, after all, Carlisle swore. She was stunned to find she wanted Tyler Carson.

If she slipped down the hall to his bedroom right now, she knew he would not turn her away. But was that the way she wanted it to be? In God's name, what was she thinking of?

She jumped off the bed and fumbled in the dark until she found her cigarettes. She had always been an occasional indulger, but knowing Tyler threatened to turn her into a chain-smoker. She got the cigarette lit on the third try. Then she stepped out on the terrace and stood smoking and staring into the night.

Some indistinct sound made her turn halfway around. She spotted the identical red glow of another cigarette twenty feet away at the other end of the long terrace that spanned the three bedrooms on this side of the house.

"Tyler?" Her voice quivered on the still night air like the tremulous flutter of a moth's wings.

"Yeah." He made no move to emerge from the shadows.

"I couldn't sleep." She swallowed, giving him an explanation he had not asked for, an explanation that was no doubt redundant under the circumstances.

Carlisle turned away from him, unaware that the pale glow of moonlight outlined her profile, the alluring curve of her firm jutting breasts, her flat abdomen, her long shapely legs.

She heard Tyler draw in his breath, sharp and harsh. "Carlisle—" Her name hovered between them like a question.

Carlisle turned to peer at Tyler's shadowy form. He took a step into the aura of light that fell from a lamp burning low somewhere in his bedroom. She could see him clearly now as he buried his cigarette in a potted plant at his elbow. He was wearing a pair of jeans and nothing else.

"Tyler—"

He jerked his head up. "Yes?"

"Would you kiss me good night?" Her voice was small, but firm.

For a moment, the man did nothing. Then barefooted, he moved stealthily, soundlessly across the terrace, rather like one of his Indian ancestors. Her heart lurched at his approach.

He stopped several feet from where she stood, never taking his eyes from her face. "I have one problem, honey, and I don't know what to do about it. I want you, Carlisle, and if I kiss you now . . ." He fell silent. The moment stretched into an eternity.

Finally, without a word, Carlisle took the last two steps into his arms. It was like coming home after a long journey. She could feel the hair on his bare chest through the thin material of her pajamas, the smooth skin of his back and shoulders beneath her touch, the jean-clad thighs that rubbed against her own. Her breasts were crushed by his weight.

"Oh, Tyler, I . . ."

"It's all right, darling. I know. Just let me hold you, kiss you—" His words were broken off, as his mouth found hers. He held back at first as if afraid his passion, unleashed to its full expression, would overwhelm her. His lips worshiped the softness of her mouth, the curve of her shoulder, the tips of her arousal that poked his skin like two hard buttons.

His hands flowed down her back until they found and cupped her rounded bottom, urging her to the knowledge that his desire for her had grown into a force he could not deny.

Then he shuddered and took a step backward. His hands dropped to his sides. "You'd better go in, Carlisle. I am trying not to take advantage of the situation, but dammit, I'm only human!" The words were bitten off sharp and terse; lines of determination and control creased the handsome face.

Carlisle studied his face, suddenly realizing she loved the way he looked—the arch of his brow, the deep glowing color of his eyes, the mole just below his left ear, the shape of his mouth, the firm but not unyielding line of his jaw. It was a face she could never tire of, a face she could live with for the rest of her life. She wanted to soothe away his tension, to hold him in her arms, to ease the loneliness of his nights.

It was one of those rare moments in time when one soul caught a glimpse of another. She knew all Tyler's strengths and weaknesses and loved them. She loved him—loved him enough to give of herself without reservation. And Lord, she needed him so!

"I don't want to go in, Tyler—not alone. I love you." There, she had finally said it, mentally burning every bridge behind her. Then she shivered, the night air chilly without the warmth of his body.

Tyler drew her through the open door and into the bedroom beyond. The small click of the lamp beside her bed was the only sound. Then he closed the terrace door partway and looked her straight in the face. He seemed to be fighting for every word. "I want to be very sure it's what we both want, Carlisle. That whatever happens, we're going into this with our eyes open. I'll leave right now if that's what you want." He was giving her an out if she wished for one and he did not try to influence her with his touch or make her tremulous with his kisses. He knew as well as she that he had only to touch her.

But Carlisle's senses were reeling with the uniquely

masculine scent he emitted. The glow of his bronze skin in the lamplight made her hands itch to touch him. Did she want to send him away now? Could she? The ache that coursed through every particle of her being shouted no. This was right for her—she knew that now with all of her heart.

She snuggled up against him, her arms snaking their way around his waist, one leg entwining his. Carlisle turned her face up to Tyler's, unafraid that her love for him shone there like a beacon. She was utterly without fear now.

"You're not going anywhere, mister—not if I have anything to say about it." Then with laughter still on her lips, she went up on her tiptoes and pressed her mouth in invitation to his.

It was an offer he could not refuse. "Oh, God, I do love you, Carly, as I've never loved another woman. I need you. You're like a hunger inside me night and day." Then the man showed her his seemingly insatiable appetite for her. His mouth trembled as it claimed hers in a kiss that soon deepened, threatening to drown them both in its ecstasy.

Their mouths came together again and again in long drugging kisses of searching hunger and rising desire. They left Carlisle's head spinning. She gave herself up to the sensations Tyler's touch was creating. She was pure emotion now, all rational thought exiled to some far corner of her mind.

With everything inside her the woman met his rising passion with her own. She eagerly opened her mouth to his, letting the taste of the man engulf her. She ran the tip of her tongue along the row of smooth white teeth, shivering as they tickled the sensitive nerves of her tongue. Caressing each lovely plane of his face, she found it was not enough. Her hands left his waist to roam at will, glorying in the hard muscular body that was so different from her own.

Then they seemed to realize they had all the time in the world to discover and explore and began to savor each kiss, each caress without hurry. Tyler pressed his lips to her eyes and nose and even the tips of her ears. He ran his hands through the mass of auburn hair, seeming to revel in the liquid fire that flowed through his fingers.

He clutched great handfuls of the stuff in his fists as if he wanted to tame its wild disarray. His mouth came down on Carlisle's, hard and masterful, the teasing quality to his kisses suddenly gone. The man drained her until she felt limp in his arms.

Tyler slipped the robe from her shoulders, letting it flutter to the carpet. His hands moved down her back, the silky material of her pajamas soft to the touch. Spanning her waist, he made his way beneath the short top, his touch like hot lava on her skin. Then his fingers found the underside of her breasts and cupped their fullness in his palms. His thumbs stroked the rosy nucleus into an erect bud, hard with desire.

"Tyler—" Carlisle moaned at the eroticism of his touch, desire curling up in her stomach.

Driven on by the look of pure sensuality that spread across her features, the man bent his head and proceeded to flick the outline of each nipple with his arrowed tongue, one after the other. She soon despaired of even the flimsy layer of material that separated them.

Wanting to give as well as receive, Carlisle placed her hands on each side of Tyler's head and drew him upright. "My turn now," she breathed in a husky voice. "I want to please you, Tyler," she murmured, running her fingertips across the muscled wall of his chest, tracing the path of golden hair that provocatively disappeared beneath the waistband of his jeans. She teased the spot where it vanished with her fingernail, while her tongue danced across his skin.

His urgent moan was her reward. It was like music to her ears. She could excite him and Carlisle loved the way that made her feel. Tyler was no easily aroused boy, but a mature, intelligent man who required that one rare woman to meet his emotional as well as his physical needs.

He reached out then to the delicate strap on each shoulder and slipped them down her arms. The top of her brief pajamas fell unheeded to their feet.

"You're the loveliest thing I've ever seen," Tyler whispered in a voice strangled by passion. One work-roughened hand reached out to caress the silky surface of her belly. A gasp escaped Carlisle's parted lips as that same hand moved up to encompass her rib cage, the other following suit. His thumbs plucked the aroused points that had flowered from their passion, so they grew dark and even harder.

A moan of intense pleasure from the woman told Tyler what he had already known. Carlisle stretched her arms above her head as he lowered his head. His mouth burned her flesh. Then he finally took her breast in his mouth, suckling at its fullness like a babe. The man consumed her, twirling his tongue in a circle, his teeth nipping at the sensitive center. Her nerves were screaming for more, for a fulfillment she could only imagine.

Tyler raised his mouth to hers once more. His tongue sought the sweetness within, extracting its nectar into himself as if it were the sustenance of life for him. "God, Carlisle, I want you!" he muttered with startling vehemence.

She could only nod her head and nuzzle her face into his neck as he drew her to the bed. She stretched out on the cool smooth sheet and watched transfixed as Tyler unzipped his jeans and slid them from his hips. He was truly wearing only the jeans. Carlisle was stunned by the sheer beauty and magnetism of the man. This was surely what man was meant to be. She reached out her arms as he came to her, welcoming his heart and soul and body with her own.

Tyler couldn't seem to get enough of her. He tasted every part of her body as though she were a cornucopia of sensual delights.

Carlisle writhed under his expert touch, ready to explode with the wondrous feelings he had revealed to her. She ran her hands down his bare thigh and across his abdomen, enjoying the feel of his body, knowing it was bringing him to a feverish pitch he sought in vain to control. She knew that Tyler wanted to be a part of her as she yearned to be one with him. She wanted to know this man as she had never known another human being, never to be totally alone again.

He prepared the way for their ultimate pleasure and ultimate union. When Carlisle was quivering with her need of him, he eased his tongue into her mouth as he slowly, gently introduced himself into her body.

As they had found each other's natural rhythm while dancing earlier that evening, so did they now, moving as one force toward their mutual satisfaction. Carlisle soon learned the ecstasy of love as her body accepted this most wonderful of changes. She whispered all that was in her heart as they ascended the heights together. For both the man and the woman it was the discovery of all that love could be and all they had ever dreamed—and more.

"Carlisle—" Her name died on his lips as he held her in the aftermath of the explosion. All he had wanted to say to her had been said with his body. The way he worshiped every detail, the pleasure he sought to give her even above his own, the gentle cherishing as well as the hunger of his need. It had all been there.

She curled up next to him, content in his arms as though she had been born to rest in them. It was thus that they drifted off to sleep the sleep of total contentment.

Carlisle was not sure what brought her back from her dreams of Tyler and the way his hands glided over her body as if he knew instinctively what pleased her most, until she awoke enough to realize he was beside her in bed, his eyes open, his hands warm and persuasive as they caressed her. She turned to him, seeking the thrill only he could give her.

Tyler impatiently threw back the sheet that partially covered them, wanting no obstacle to his view of her long, lithe body. He lay on his side, his head resting on the pillow, allowing his fingers to touch each spot where his eyes fell. He started with her face, tracing each feature with a feather-light caress. He circled her mouth with his thumb until she impishly caught it between her teeth and pressed down hard. Her newly acquired knowledge told her that the line between pain and pleasure was infinitesimally close.

"Ouch!" Tyler jerked his finger away, pretending an injury.

"Surely that didn't hurt a big strong man like you." She laughed as she nudged his hand back toward her. She held it up to the light and methodically kissed each finger in turn, then teased his palm with darting flicks of her tongue.

"I do believe you're going to be a very apt pupil, Miss Scott," he murmured, in a voice that said her every move pleased him.

"Oh, really." She sniffed indignantly. "And I suppose you fancy yourself the teacher."

The man grinned broadly. "That thought had occurred to me."

"You're not the only fish in the sea, Tyler Carson!" she returned flippantly.

"I better be as far as you're concerned, honey." His tone was gruff as he rolled over on top of her, pinning her to the bed with his body. "I'm a jealous man, Carlisle. What is mine, I keep, and you would do well to remember that."

Carlisle impudently stuck her tongue out at the man, only to discover he would brook no rebellion on her part. His mouth smothered hers in a punishing kiss as she twisted and turned under him. Like a trapped animal that recognized the victor, she went limp beneath his weight. Tyler momentarily relaxed his hold, not realizing what she was up to. The woman maneuvered herself until one hand was freed. It was that hand she brought down now with a resounding slap on his buttocks.

The look of utter surprise on his face set Carlisle to laughing. It began as a tremor and then broke into a self-satisfied chuckle as it surfaced on her lips.

"What in the hell did you do that for?" Tyler brought his face within an inch of hers, the light of desire rekindling in his eyes.

"I don't know," she stammered, biting her lip and looking all of twelve. "I seem to recall reading in one of 'those' magazines that it's supposed to be considered erotic."

"*This* is erotic," said the man as he directed her hands in a way that was pleasing to him, while his own found the feminine counterpart of this pleasure in a lazy massaging action that quickly had her begging for more, though no words passed her lips.

Tyler hovered above her for a moment, denying them both what they wanted most. Carlisle arched her hips toward the man's body, trying to capture the elusive release that only he could provide. Yet he stalled longer, teasing her. She felt the anticipatory excitement and warmth spread through her lower torso as his fingers launched their invasion. Her face flushed with a desire that mounted again and again to his caress until the moment of sweet release set her free.

The woman gazed up at him shyly. "Tyler . . ." The words stuck in her throat.

"I love you, Carly, and you love me. Anything between us is good and right. You don't know how it makes me feel when you tremble at my touch. Oh, babe . . ." And with that he could deny himself no longer, but began anew to seduce her to a quivering mass of flesh.

This time their bodies met in a volcanic explosion that threatened their very sanity. Carlisle frantically clung to him, the way still unfamiliar. She scaled the heights of passion time after time, until Tyler joined her at last for the final climb together. It was some time before either of them was capable of speaking and then it was in hushed, awed tones.

"I-I didn't realize it could be like that," she confessed, burying her face in his shoulder.

"It can be for some people, if they're very lucky," Tyler said, wonder in his voice. "You must know now that we were meant for each other, Carlisle." He did not bother to disguise his pleasure.

"Meant for each other . . ." she repeated, as sleep once again overtook her.

From long years of habit, Tyler Carson awoke at first light of day. He lay still for several minutes, knowing with his body if not his mind that some momentous change had taken place in his life. Then his gaze fell on the face beside his, still soft and innocent in sleep as it was. The man felt desire stir in his loins as the memory of their night of love flooded his consciousness. Visions of awakening Carlisle with his kiss filled his mind to the exclusion of all else. Would he ever get enough of her? Tyler knew the answer was no, that he would only desire her more and more each time they made love.

As he moved toward the sleeping form, intent on attaining his objective, the man became aware of a faint knock at the door of his own bedroom just down the hall.

He froze, listening for the knock to be repeated and heard his name as well. It was Rosemary Quinn.

Having no wish to embarrass his housekeeper or Carlisle, Tyler slipped off the bed and scooped up his jeans. With the swiftness of a deer, he was out the french doors, down the length of the terrace, and into his own room in a matter of seconds. He paused to catch his breath, pressing his chin against the hard wooden door.

"Tyler . . ." Rosemary repeated the knock louder this time.

"Yes?" He finally found his voice.

"I'm sorry to disturb you, but Lew Hanken is on the telephone."

Tyler swore under his breath. Not now—God, not now! "Did he say what he wanted, Rosemary?" He tried to keep the irritation he was feeling out of his voice. Hopping first on one foot and then the other, he pulled the jeans over his hips. He reached for a shirt that hung over the back of the chair at his elbow.

"Lew said to tell you they found a dozen head of cattle in a patch of locoweed this morning."

"Damn!" The word broke from his lips as he swung the bedroom door open. "Sorry, Rosemary, but it's a hell of a way to start the day."

"I know, Tyler," she murmured sympathetically.

"Did Lew say he needed to talk to me?"

"No, he said he'd meet you out in the north range whenever you could get there."

Tyler threaded his fingers through his tousled brown hair. "All right, tell him I'll be there in an hour," he stated brusquely, resigned to the fact that business came before pleasure.

"Sure thing. I'll go right down to the kitchen and see to your breakfast." Rosemary wrapped her blue cotton robe closer about her as she spoke.

"Thanks, Rosemary," he murmured with real affection.

"I'm just sorry I had to wake you up, Tyler. I was hoping you could sleep in a bit this morning."

"So was I," he replied passionately. "So was I."

6

The intense glare of the midmorning sun roused Carlisle from sleep. Not the slightest sound of anyone stirring could be detected within the house. With toes pointed and arms raised high above her head, she stretched her body in a long lazy catlike movement. Then remembering the previous night, she turned over to stare at the empty pillow beside her, not the least surprised to find she was alone. Just because she didn't have to work on this glorious Saturday morning did not mean the operation of the ranch stopped. Still, she would have preferred to awaken in the arms of the man she had loved with her heart, mind, and body the night before.

Carlisle hugged the memory of their lovemaking to her like a mantle of warm fur. She lazily slid out of bed, regarding her own nakedness without a shred of self-consciousness. Her bare feet pattered across the tiled floor of the bathroom as she reached in to adjust the flow and temperature of the shower. A little off-key, she burst into the chorus of "Some Enchanted Evening."

She took her time showering and drying her hair. Every routine seemed to take on new meaning this morning. This was the hair Tyler adored running his hands through, she mused as she brushed it to a flowing sheen. Every inch of her was vitally alive as she stepped into lacy underthings and a one-piece jump suit that buttoned up the front. The tiny buttons ran all the way to the throat, but she impulsively left several undone. Tying the matching belt around her waist, Carlisle could almost imagine the feel of Tyler's incredibly strong hands spanning her middle. She strapped her feet into leather sandals in the same shade of pale sunflower yellow as the jump suit.

Applying a touch of makeup to her face, she smiled bemusedly at her reflection in the bathroom mirror. "You do look like the self-satisfied cat who's had her cream, my dear."

At the reference to cream, Carlisle suddenly realized she was ravenously hungry. She traipsed downstairs and found the uninhabited kitchen in perfect order. Putting the kettle on the stove to heat, she helped herself to a cup and a tea bag from the cupboard.

"Forgive the intrusion, Rosemary," she murmured to the absent housekeeper, "but I'm starved!"

Carlisle proceeded to rummage about the kitchen until she located bread, eggs, milk, and butter—all the makings of the french toast she fully intended having for her breakfast.

She had just taken a whisk from the bowl of milk and

eggs when she heard the kitchen door swing open behind her. The dazzling smile quickly faded from her eyes and mouth as she saw the all too familiar swath of black hair that belonged to Maria Chavez. Twenty-nine years of proper upbringing forbade her to simply ignore the girl, but her greeting was barely civil at that. "Good morning, Maria." She turned back to her task, beating the eggs with unnecessary vigor.

"H-hello, Miss Scott," the girl responded, without her usual brashness, or so it seemed to Carlisle.

"I'm afraid you've made a wasted trip. Tyler isn't here."

"Yes, I know. I saw Rosemary before she left to do her shopping this morning." Maria advanced several steps into the room. She seemed younger somehow in a print sundress and low-heeled sandals, her face scrubbed clean of makeup. "Actually, I came to see you, Miss Scott. I-I want to apologize for the way I behaved last night." Her voice quivered with uncertainty. "I know I was unforgivably rude and I just wanted to say that I'm sorry." Her dark head was bent, but the words were clearly spoken.

Carlisle slowly put the bowl down on the counter and turned around. The girl raised eyes bright with unshed tears to meet hers.

"I was jealous of you. I realize that now. You're beautiful and intelligent and grown up, and Tyler finds you interesting. . . ." Maria ran out of breath for a moment.

Just how interesting the girl would never know, Carlisle thought wryly to herself.

"Anyway, I wanted Tyler to see me as a woman,

too—the-the way he does you. I haven't been very nice to you since you arrived and I apologize for that. I wish we could be friends, Miss Scott. Do you think we might be?" Maria was practically pleading with her now.

Carlisle felt her anger melt away. She'd always been a soft touch and after all, Maria was scarcely more than a child. Jealousy was a potent force for a young woman going through the throes of her first crush on an older man. She could understand the attraction Tyler held for Maria. She found him rather irresistible herself. It had been a brave thing for Maria to come to her like this.

"Apology accepted," Carlisle responded. "I was just about to fix myself some french toast and a cup of tea," she explained. "Would you care to join me?"

"I've had breakfast, Miss Scott, but a cup of tea would be nice," the girl answered politely.

She marveled at the change in Maria. The girl was quite a nice young thing when she wished to be.

"If we're going to be friends, then I think you should call me Carlisle," she stated, getting another cup from the kitchen shelf.

"All right—Carlisle." Maria tried the name out, obviously pleased by the honor bestowed on her.

Perhaps she had been partly to blame, Carlisle thought. If she had been kinder, had treated Maria more like an adult and less like a child, they might have been friends sooner. Well, at least they were starting out on the right foot now.

She flipped two pieces of french toast, browned to perfection, onto a plate. "Are you sure you won't join me?"

"No, thank you, just tea is fine," the younger woman

replied. "By the way, I almost forgot—Rosemary asked me to tell you that Tyler was called away early this morning. There was some kind of emergency up on the north range. It seems a few head of cattle got into some locoweed."

"Is that bad?" Carlisle inquired between bites.

"You really are a gringo, aren't you?" Maria's laugh echoed with traces of her former disparagement. "Locoweed is poisonous to cattle." She straightened up in the chair, gazing into the bottom of her teacup. "Rosemary said Tyler didn't expect to be back until dinnertime." For a fleeting moment her mouth formed a hard unyielding line in her face. "What are you planning to do today, Carlisle?" she inquired, as if it were of genuine interest to her.

"I don't know." Carlisle's fork stopped in midair. "Maybe I'll take in a few of the local sights. I've been here a month and all I've seen is this ranch house and the dam site—oh, and your parents' lovely home, of course," she quickly corrected herself, thinking her oversight might sound rude.

"Say—you're an engineer, right?" Maria Chavez obviously had something in mind.

"Right." She glanced up with curiosity.

"Well, supposedly one of the most remarkable engineering feats in the West isn't too far from here—up by E-town."

"Elizabethtown? I believe George Henson mentioned it last night at the party."

"Yes, Elizabethtown. Of course, it's a ghost town now, but back before the Civil War it was the biggest gold-producing area in New Mexico." Maria recited her history with enthusiasm. "Anyway, they built this water system for the mines called the Big Ditch. I was thinking since you're an engineer and all—well, if you are interested, I can give you directions."

"Why, thank you, Maria. Would you like to come along with me?" Carlisle made the offer in good faith.

"It's nice of you to ask me, but—well, I promised my mother I would help her this afternoon. It's not hard to find if you'd like to go," the girl stammered, her face oddly animated and tinged with pink.

"I think I will," Carlisle said adventurously, her interest piqued by Maria's commentary. "I'll just wash up my dishes and get a few things from my room. You can give me directions if you will."

"Let me wash those for you, Carlisle." A small hand intervened, removing the kitchen sponge from hers. "You go ahead and get your things."

Carlisle tried to hide her surprise. "Thank you, Maria," she murmured, glancing back over her shoulder as she left the kitchen. The girl was softly humming to herself as she tidied the counter.

When Carlisle returned to the kitchen a quarter of an hour later it was in perfect order and Maria was just screwing the top on a thermos bottle.

"I thought you might get thirsty," she said shyly, holding the thermos out to the woman. "It's iced tea."

"How nice! Thank you, Maria." Carlisle was touched by the girl's thoughtfulness. At the last minute she added an apple from the refrigerator. Just in case she got hungry. Then with her cap jauntily perched on her head and her camera slung over her shoulder, she stowed her few supplies in the front seat of the Jeep.

"Go back out to Highway 85 and turn north," instructed the girl. "Once you get past Springer, go west to Eagle Nest. Elizabethtown is just down the road from there. You can't miss it." Maria stepped back from the Jeep and waved.

"Thanks!" Carlisle shouted back gaily. Then she seemed to hesitate. "You know, it looks kind of dark over there." She pointed toward the northwest.

"Just a few harmless clouds," reassured her self-appointed guide. "They're not unusual around here this time of year."

"Well, thanks again, Maria. I'm glad we're going to be friends now." Carlisle gave the girl a parting smile and drove off.

"Yes, thanks a lot, Maria," Carlisle muttered as she carefully maneuvered the vehicle along State Highway 38 toward the deserted E-town.

The going had been longer and rougher than the girl had indicated, that was for sure. The uncharitable thought crossed Carlisle's mind that the omission may have been deliberate. But the glorious view from the mountain road made even that omission of secondary importance. She knew now why New Mexico was called the "Land of Enchantment," for it was that indeed.

She reached back and rubbed the spot on her neck that had begun to ache in earnest a half hour ago. It occurred to her then that she should have left some kind of note for Rosemary as to her whereabouts. Oh, well, it was too late for that now. She would simply have to be back at Chula Vista before anyone missed her.

Carlisle drove around the range of towering peaks and

there, nestled against the side of the next mountain and down into the valley, were the crumbling deserted buildings that had once been a thriving mining town. Elizabethtown. Suddenly it didn't matter whether Maria Chavez had been playing a bad joke on her or not. She was thoroughly entranced.

She pulled off the road and found a nice shady, protected spot for the Jeep. As she gazed up the length of the hill in front of her she was very glad she had thought to change from her rather flimsy sandals into hiking boots. The ground here was fairly well overgrown with scrub and tall grass.

Grabbing her camera and eager now to get started, Carlisle set out on the long hike up the first hill. She passed several ramshackle cabins, peering inside with care, for their roofs sagged ominously. Along the way she paused to snap particularly picturesque scenes with her camera. Here was a boarded-up storefront, the lettering above its door faded by the ravages of time and nature. She encountered the stark stone ruins of what she imagined to have once been E-town's hotel. And farther along she discovered remnants of trestles and hand-riveted pipe, which she deduced to be the remains of the Big Ditch. She lingered there for some time, amazed by the ingenuity of those early forerunners of her own profession.

The hillsides of Elizabethtown, though deserted by man, were covered with a profusion of wild flowers. The visitor was momentarily tempted to pick an armful, until she realized that they would be no more than wilted remains by the time she got back to Chula Vista.

Carlisle stood atop the highest hill and drank in the

sweeping panorama and intoxicating scents. Bees buzzed about their business while flocks of birds flew overhead. This was nature as it should be, she mused. In years to come all signs of man would crumble into dust and disappear and this land would again become what it once was.

She tried to recall the word she had once heard in reference to a ghost town—a town whose reason for existence had long since evaporated, blown away by the wind, washed away by the rain. What had it been? "Helldorados"—that was it—helldorados.

Carlisle savored this time alone, so unlike the loneliness that had threatened to engulf her these past few weeks. The feeling of restlessness was gone—gone in the wake of her budding love affair with Tyler. She closed her eyes for a moment, felt a gentle breeze stir the wisps of hair about her face that had come loose from the makeshift ponytail.

"Tyler," she whispered his name to a wild clover. "Tyler Carson—I love you!" she shouted to a gnarled, bent tree, feeling rather silly and schoolgirlish for giving in to the impulse. She quickly looked about her to see if anyone had heard, which was even sillier since she was all alone up here on the mountain.

Discovering a patch of soft grass that had not grown as tall as the grass on the hillside, she flopped down on the carpet provided by nature. She lay back and exhaled a long contented sigh.

At peace with herself for the first time in she knew not how long, the woman let her mind wander at will. In that elusive half-world between wakefulness and sleep, she could conjure up the image of Tyler as clearly as if he were actually there beside her. Carlisle could feel his touch at her throat, teasing the tip of her breast as it peaked through the top of her jump suit, caressing the soft sensitive skin of her inner thigh. She had fantasized in the past about how it would be with a man, but no amount of fantasizing had prepared her for the reality of love. The reality was far better than the dream. She knew that now.

But she would be leaving New Mexico in another two months and then what? What would become of her and Tyler Carson? Suddenly the thought of leaving him plunged her into a dark pit of depression. She was in love with the man. In only a few short weeks he had become as necessary to her as breathing. Fear clutched at her heart. This then was the pain of loving—not the loss of pride she had felt at Wade's defection—but this rapier-sharp thrust to the very center of her being.

"Tyler . . ." His name was torn from her throat. Carlisle sat up with a start. "Tyler!" Her cry was lost in the wind, as the first resounding clap of thunder echoed through the valley below.

She looked around her, startled to find that dark turbulent clouds, angry giants in the sky, had swiftly moved into the area while her attention was on the rancher. She continued to sit there for a minute or two before realizing the seriousness of the situation. Another crack of thunder sounded nearby.

"Better make a run for it, Carlisle, or you are going to get a bit damp!" she said aloud, as if hearing her own voice were preferable to hearing none at all.

The woman pressed the camera to her breast and began to run down the mountainside. The going was necessarily slow for she did not want to do something stupid like stumble and fall. Her long legs loped along like a gazelle in motion.

The Jeep was in full view when she did the very thing she had been trying to avoid. For one brief moment Carlisle took her eyes off the ground. The next thing she knew she was flat on her face, dirt in her mouth, burrs tugging at her hair and clothes, small cuts stinging her hands and elbows where they scraped the rocky hillside.

"Damn!" She cursed her own clumsiness. "OH!" she cried out again, grasping her ankle. A pain shot through her foot when she attempted to move it.

Carlisle put her head down on her hands until the wave of nausea passed. By now the rain was pelting her back like hundreds of bits of hard cold hail. For a second she gave in to despair, a low animal moan issuing from her lips only to be lost in the percussion of nature's symphony. But the woman recognized that self-pity was not going to help her, nor would it get her in from the drenching rain. It was coming down now in a long gray sheet.

She propped herself up and, with the aid of a broken tree branch, managed to get to her feet. With teeth clenched until she was sure her lip must be bleeding, and with frequent rest stops, Carlisle limped her way to the Jeep. Rain ran down her cheeks and into her eyes and nose and mouth. Her hair was matted to her neck and shoulders like an uncomfortably heavy mantle of wet fur. The jump suit clung to her body like a second skin.

She tore the door of the Jeep open and braced herself for the pain she knew would strike once she put her weight on her foot.

"Damn!" she hissed, flinching at the sharp pain that seemed to rack her entire body. "Damn you, Maria Chavez! Damn you, Tyler Carson! Damn you all!" Carlisle sobbed as she collapsed over the steering wheel. She reached out blindly and pulled the door closed behind her.

A few meaningless clouds? It was suddenly black as night—a night without moon or stars to light the way. The very mountains were alive with electricity. They shuddered and groaned as though the bowels of the earth would open wide and swallow them whole. Carlisle was both fascinated and terrified by the spectacular unfolding before her eyes, humbled by the display of nature's power. Then a crackle of lightning struck directly overhead and for the first time she was genuinely afraid.

The woman courageously straighened up, mopping the tears and rain from her face as best she could. Crying would get her absolutely nowhere, she reasoned. She was cold and wet and hungry, and wished she had thought to bring some kind of jacket with her—but uppermost in her mind was to get away from this place as fast as was humanly possible.

Carlisle hopefully turned the key in the ignition. Her hopes faltered as the Jeep sputtered and strained with the effort and finally died. She took a deep breath and tried again, but still the Jeep wouldn't budge. Her heart began to beat erratically. She was forced to remind herself to stay calm. With the third unsuccessful attempt, she had to face the fact that she wasn't going anywhere—not now and not in this Jeep.

But hope dies hard and Carlisle reasoned if she could keep panic at bay, patience would pay off in the end. She sat there clutching the steering wheel until her knuckles were white. She tried not to dwell on the fact that she was stranded in the middle of nowhere with a storm raging outside. She was feeling miserable, too. There were rather nasty scrapes on her hands and arms. Her ankle was sprained, or at the least badly twisted, although that was strictly a self-diagnosis. There was little doubt as to the throbbing in her head and the matter of a Jeep that refused to start.

Lightning flashed all around like a wizard's fury. Thunder rolled across the valley with a cannon's boom. The woman cringed in one corner of the vehicle, the arms wrapped about her of little comfort. She remembered then the story her father had told her when she was a small child. During the worst of the storm he would make her laugh by telling her that thunder was simply God rolling potatoes out of a barrel. There had been plenty of storms back in the Midwest when she was a girl, but there had always been a certain security in huddling with her family by the cellar door. She hadn't been alone then—not like she was now.

Tentatively, and with a hastily said prayer on her lips, Carlisle once again turned the key in the ignition. Nothing happened. Not the faintest sound could be discerned, the slightest movement felt. The woman fell back against the seat and began to laugh. It started out as a high trill in the back of her throat and then moved to the front of her mouth and grew into a full hysterical laugh. She was really in a pickle this time. Hot stinging tears raced down her face as she promptly burst into a good long cry.

The hours dragged on and still the storm did not subside. Carlisle's nerves were frayed to a raw edge. She tried to concentrate on happier days with her family, of loving moments spent in Tyler's embrace, even reciting trigonometric logarithms—all to no avail.

Every crescendo sent a scream of terror spiraling to her mouth. She was physically and emotionally beyond exhaustion and yet sleep evaded her. A trembling prayer of entreaty formed on lips pinched and blue with cold. Dry sobs shook her body. She leaned her forehead on the steering wheel and closed her eyes at last.

The man burst in the back door of the ranch house and stood there for a moment watching the rain pour in a brown stream from his hat and poncho onto the immaculate kitchen floor. Rosemary wouldn't be pleased, he remarked to himself. He was making a god-awful mess of things.

"Rosemary!" he bellowed like an exasperated bull. "Get me a couple of old towels, will you?"

The housekeeper scurried into the room, a stack of towels under her arm. "My, but you are a sight!" She clucked her tongue in disapproval as only she could.

"I know . . . I know . . ." Tyler muttered, rubbing his head with one of the terrycloth towels she handed him. "Don't scold, Rosemary. It's been a hell of a day! I'm cold and wet and hungry. All I want right now is a hot shower and a good belt of whiskey in that order."

"But—Tyler."

"Not now, Rosemary." He threw the towel down on the bench and marched into his study, slamming the door behind him none too gently.

The woman stood there for a moment, concern darkening her blue eyes to the color of midnight. Oh, well, at this point what were a few more minutes one way or the other? She would tell Tyler after he had showered.

Rosemary Quinn was waiting for him when he reappeared fifteen minutes later.

"I feel like a new man." Tyler gave her an apologetic grin. "Sorry I was short-tempered earlier. We had quite a time of it with those cattle, and then this damned storm blew in." The man shook his head as much to say there were some days he just couldn't win.

"Tyler . . ."

He looked around the kitchen inquiringly. "What's for supper? I'm starving. Where's Carlisle?"

The housekeeper wrung her hands in agitation. "That's what I've been trying to tell you. I haven't seen Carlisle all day and the Jeep is missing."

"What the hell do you mean the Jeep is missing?" he demanded violently.

"I mean the Jeep was gone when I got home from shopping and so was Carlisle. I haven't seen either since." Worried though she was, Rosemary told her story in clear, concise terms.

Tyler's mouth drew into a tight line. "Wasn't Carlisle up when you left this morning?"

The housekeeper denied this with a shake of her head. "No. The poor thing's looked so tired lately that I hated to wake her."

A pained expression flickered across the man's features. Carlisle was gone—that was what registered in his mind. He turned abruptly and stomped out of the kitchen. When he got to the stairs, he took them two at a time, not stopping to catch his breath until the door to her bedroom crashed open under the impact of his weight.

A quick survey of the room satisfied the man that nothing *seemed* out of place. Tyler crossed to the closet and flung it open. All of Carlisle's things were still there. In a way he was relieved. For just a moment, he had feared that the events of the previous night might have driven her away. Apparently, that wasn't so. With a painful shrug of his broad shoulders, he closed the door and retraced his steps to the kitchen.

"All of her things are still there," the housekeeper stated, as if that, too, had been her first thought.

"Where could the little fool have gone?" the man hissed. His face was tired and drawn in lines of heavy concentration. "Did she leave a note?" He fought to sound neutral as he asked.

"No . . ." the woman paused thoughtfully, "but Maria might know something."

"Maria!" Tyler exclaimed sharply, his brows contracted into a scowl. "What does Maria have to do with this?"

"Perhaps nothing, but she did come by to see Carlisle this morning as I was leaving," Rosemary said matter-of-factly.

Tyler was already dialing the telephone in his study before the woman finished speaking. Rosemary quietly followed him into the room, worry lines crisscrossing her face. She stationed herself by the desk and waited.

"Hello, Ramón. This is Tyler. I need to speak with Maria. It's important." He impatiently tapped the receiver as he waited for the girl to come to the telephone. "Maria? I understand you saw Miss Scott this morning. Well, she's missing along with her Jeep. Did she say anything to you about where she was headed? . . . What do you mean you're not sure?" Tyler said tersely. "Either she did or she didn't. Well, didn't you tell her there was a storm warning out?" He turned to the housekeeper. "Maria says Carlisle mentioned something about seeing the local sights." Tyler jerked his attention back to the telephone. "I want you to tell me every word Carlisle said to you, Maria." His voice was stern, demanding that she answer him. "Elizabethtown? All the way up there?" Horror filled the man's voice. "Okay, niña, I'm sure you did your best. Thanks." He curtly concluded their conversation.

Tyler put the receiver down and stood there for a moment, running his hands through his hair in agitation. When he faced Rosemary there was a cold fear in his manner.

"Maria said Carlisle mentioned something about going up to E-Town. She tried to discourage her from going, but Carlisle was adamant. God, Rosemary—she could be stranded up in those mountains!" He swore softly under his breath.

The woman stared at him with sudden comprehension. "Look, Carlisle is an intelligent woman. I'm sure she would have the sense to seek shelter when the storm came up." She tried her best to sound reassuring, but the quiver in her voice gave the housekeeper away.

"You're worried about her, too, aren't you?" he said in a slurred tone, obviously voicing the words with difficulty.

"Yes—yes, I am," she confessed.

"She could be hurt or something may have happened to the Jeep. . . ." Tyler's tongue was thick in his mouth. He stood there poised for a minute. "I have to go after her, Rosemary."

"Of course, you do. I'll get together a thermos of hot

127

coffee and some sandwiches. You may need them if—when you find Carlisle. She's bound to be pretty hungry." The woman brushed away the two tears she had allowed herself and bustled into the kitchen.

"Thanks, Rosemary." Tyler went into action as well, gathering several blankets and dry ponchos which he stacked on the kitchen table. He mentally clicked off the supplies he carried in the pickup—flashlight, rope, first-aid kit. With the box of food from Rosemary, he made several trips to the truck, loading everything quickly and efficiently.

"Take care of yourself, Tyler," the woman implored, as he left for the last time. "Some of those mountain roads could be washed out with all this rain."

"I'll be fine," he muttered as he pulled the Stetson down over his eyes. Or at least he would be once he found Carlisle, he told himself.

7

She must have dozed off, for when Carlisle awakened later she had an uncanny sense that some time had passed. She tried to peer at the face of her wristwatch, holding it up to catch the light from the storm that still ricocheted back and forth between the mountaintops. She finally caught a glimpse of the dial. It read five o'clock. That was impossible, she reasoned. It had to be hours past five. She put the watch up to her ear, but could detect no ticking. The darned thing had stopped; she grimaced. No doubt in the tumble she had taken down the hillside or in the drenching she had received. Either way, it too had quit on her.

She stretched out her long legs, noting quite objectively that the pain in her ankle seemed subdued. She ran a hand down the muscle to her foot, finding it puffy and swollen. She was tempted to remove the hiking boot to give it some relief until she thought better of it. She'd never get the boot back on if she took it off now.

Lord, she was famished, Carlisle acknowledged. Then she remembered the apple she had stuck in the glove compartment of the Jeep just in case she got hungry that afternoon. Thank heaven for small favors, she mused, reaching across to extract it. She leaned her head back against the seat and took small purposeful nibbles of the apple, chewing every bite for all it was worth. Under the circumstances, she felt half now and half later would be a wise course to follow.

Carlisle had returned the uneaten portion to the glove box and was sitting there with her eyes closed to shut out the sight of the storm, when the door of the Jeep was yanked open.

She nearly jumped out of her skin. Her scream of utter terror was drowned out by a loud rumble of thunder overhead. A flash of lightning revealed an apparition looming before her like some menacing dark giant. A bright beam of light blinded her. Only one thought formed in Carlisle's mind, one word on her lips. Her voice rose in a tremendous crescendo.

"TY—LER!" she screamed, with every ounce of breath in her body.

"Carlisle—dammit, honey, it *is* me!" The apparition shook the woman until her teeth rattled.

Tyler? She formed his name, but no sound would come out. "Tyler?" This time it was loud and clear. Carlisle propelled herself out of the Jeep and into his arms, practically knocking the man over, the pain in her ankle all but forgotten.

"You crazy little fool, you're going to get all wet!" he

mouthed, turning her around and shoving her back into the Jeep.

Carlisle scooted across to the passenger's side as Tyler climbed in behind the wheel. He set the flashlight down and pulled the door closed. Then in one fluid movement, Tyler's hat and poncho went over his head and into the back of the vehicle.

Carlisle went into his arms without a word, needing his strength to make her feel whole again.

"God, honey—I hope I never have to live through another night like this one! I-I . . ." The man was rendered speechless, unable to find the words to describe the cold empty fear that had crept into his soul, that had hardened his heart to stone when he had found her gone.

Their eyes met—both dark, disturbed, still bracketed with the pain each had experienced when they realized how easily their first of night of love could also have been their last.

Then their mouths came together in an eruption of feelings. Desperation mingled with desire as they reached for each other. Tyler's lips were hard and forceful on hers, as if all gentleness had been wrung from his body. He bruised her lips again and again until Carlisle was sure they were swollen with his frenzied kisses. But she didn't care. She would take this kind of punishment any day of the week.

The man's hands moved convulsively over her body, wanting to know that every bone and muscle was still in its proper place. Carlisle found her own hands seeking to touch him everywhere at once, as if to prove to herself he was not an apparition, after all.

Mutual pain soon became mutual passion as the search continued. Tyler grunted impatiently, struggling with the row of tiny buttons that ran down the front of her jump suit. Several buttons popped off and rolled onto the floor, before Carlisle stopped to help him find the way to the smooth expanse of bare skin between her breasts. He buried his mouth against her with an anguished groan.

Then the man went stiff in her arms. He raised his head and looked her straight in the eyes, his own still clouded by desire. "Hell, honey—I'm too old to make love in the front seat of a Jeep like some damned acrobatic teenager!" Tyler sat back, wiping the beads of perspiration from his upper lip.

Carlisle took a deep breath and let him go. Tyler was real and he was here! She put her head on his shoulder and exhaled a sigh of relief. Whatever happened now she knew it would be all right.

She nuzzled her mouth close to his ear. "Can we go home now?" she asked in a sleep-sounding voice. She saw him mouth "hell, no," as another clap of thunder shook the valley.

Once the din had subsided, Tyler spelled it out for her loud and clear. "We can't go back tonight. I was lucky to get this far with flash floods washing out parts of the mountain roads. We'll have to wait until daylight and pray this rain lets up. God, you're frozen!" he exclaimed, as undisguised tremors ran through her.

Carlisle could only nod, her teeth literally chattering in her head.

Tyler gently did up the remaining buttons of her jump suit. "Look, we're going to have to go back out in that stuff, Carlisle. We have to find some kind of shelter where

I can get a fire started. You can't sit here all night in those damp clothes." He studied the pale face of the woman beside him, keeping his own feelings of rage and impotency at bay through sheer willpower. Carlisle needed his cool head now. He couldn't afford to be angry—not yet. "Well, are you game?" He gave her an encouraging smile.

"I-I'm g-game." She shuddered.

"Good girl!" Tyler reached across and planted a hard swift kiss on her mouth. "There are a few supplies I want to get in the pickup. Rosemary sent hot coffee and sandwiches. She figured you'd be pretty hungry by the time I found you."

Carlisle tried to give him a smile in return. "I-I'm starving."

"I'll go get the other poncho I brought along and then we can carry the stuff up to one of those cabins. All right?" He retrieved his Stetson and poncho from behind him.

"Tyler—" She hated what she had to tell him now.

The man turned around. "Yes?"

"I-ah-I twisted my ankle. It's all swollen. I don't think I can walk on it without help," she confessed in a small voice.

"Oh, hon, how did you do that to yourself?"

Carlisle bent her head so the man had to strain to hear her. "I fell down the hill." She choked back a sob.

"It's all right, Carly. I'll get you to a shelter first and then go back for the supplies. You stay put while I get the poncho." Tyler threw the door open and vanished into the night.

The woman hoisted herself back into the driver's seat

and waited for his return. It seemed like an hour, but it could only have been a matter of minutes before the Jeep door was flung wide and Tyler was fitting the garment over her head.

"Ready to give it a try?" he asked, smoothing the hair back from her face and settling her cap firmly on her head.

"Ready as I'll ever be," she answered, gritting her teeth as she eased her weight onto the injured foot.

Tyler put an arm around her waist to take most of her weight on himself. The rain was still coming down in buckets. Rivulets ran off the brim of his cowboy hat to wash down his shoulders. Side by side the couple trudged up the hill, the flashlight rather inadequately showing them the way.

The man poked his head in the first cabin they came to and flashed the beam of light around its walls. "No good," he reported. "The roof looks like it could cave in any minute."

Carlisle nodded, stumbling along beside him to the next structure.

"Wait here," he instructed, propping her against the door for support. He moved about the room, double-checking for leaks and structural weaknesses. He even poked his head in the fireplace and rummaged about for a minute. "I think this one should do," he finally announced, helping her inside.

"It's in surprisingly good shape," Carlisle stated in a cheerful voice, trying to bolster her own spirits as much as Tyler's. But she couldn't help but peer into the shrouded corners of the room, wondering what creatures stirred there.

Tyler slipped the rain-soaked poncho over her head and spread it out on the floor next to the fireplace. "You sit there while I get a fire going," he said, stripping off his own poncho and hat.

With the resounding crack of splintering wood, he broke board after board over his knee and stacked them in the grate. He added a few smaller pieces of wood and a bit of cloth he'd found somewhere in the cabin's debris. Taking a lighter from his shirt pocket, he set flame to the wood. Once he seemed satisfied the fire was going, Tyler pulled his poncho back on and walked over to where Carlisle sat staring into the flickering light. "You'll be all right here. Just stay by the fire. I'll be back in a few minutes with the supplies." He touched his hand to her face. "I'll be back, Carlisle—I promise."

She had not meant to let him see the fear in her face. She knew he had to go and yet she wanted him to stay. She was behaving like a frightened child, not a full-grown woman, Carlisle admonished herself. "I'll be fine." She gave Tyler a smile to prove it.

"Right! Keep the home fires burning, sweetheart." With a tip of his Stetson, the man was out the door and gone.

Carlisle could not have said with any confidence how long it was before the cabin door slammed open to readmit Tyler. She did know she'd never been so happy to see someone in her entire life. He had a cache of supplies rolled in a blanket tucked under the waterproof tarp. She watched with fascination as he opened the makeshift knapsack and began methodically removing item after item. There was a first-aid kit, a large thermos —presumably the coffee Rosemary had sent along, a packet of sandwiches, two dry blankets, a length of rope, and a pack of cigarettes. He had thought of everything.

He spread his poncho across a rickety old table that had only two remaining legs. He secured the length of rope in a temporary clothesline across one end of the cabin. Then he held out one of the blankets to Carlisle. "You better get out of those wet clothes and wrap yourself in this," he suggested.

"Thank you," she murmured, in a half whisper. She turned away from him and began to undo the buttons down the front of her jump suit. Her fingers, numb with cold as they were, found the simple task surprisingly difficult. With that finally accomplished, Carlisle bent her left leg and attempted to ease the boot off her injured foot. "Ow!" The moan involuntarily slipped past her lips.

"Let me do that," Tyler said, going down on his haunches in front of her. "Brace yourself, Carly. This could hurt."

She leaned her head against the rough cabin wall as he untied first one boot and then the other and slipped them off her feet. Next he dispensed with her rain-soaked socks, his fingers brushing along her bare skin in the process. Carlisle shivered at his touch in spite of herself.

"Good Lord, Carlisle! Those are some nasty scrapes you have there," he muttered, holding her hands up to the firelight. "As soon as you've undressed, I better put some antiseptic on those and wrap your ankle."

"Yessir, Doctor Carson!" she mumbled under her breath. "I'm so hungry I could eat a cow. When do we get to have some sandwiches and coffee?" she asked in a louder voice.

"Just as soon as you take your clothes off," he replied without batting an eye.

The woman quirked an eyebrow in his direction. "Is that a proposition, Mr. Carson?"

An ironic smile framed his mouth. "I'm glad to see you haven't lost your sense of humor. Can you manage the rest on your own?"

"Yes, thank you," she replied politely, suppressing the temptation to say no, thinking of the feel of his hands on her flesh if she only dared. But last night's intimacy seemed far away at the moment.

Tyler grunted and moved away from her, affording her the privacy he felt she required.

Carlisle slipped the jump suit from her shoulders and tugged the clinging material down over her hips. It lay in a wet heap at her feet. She unhooked her bra and let it drop on top of the jump suit. She hesitated, then added her wet panties. Leaning over to pick up the blanket, she wrapped it around her shoulders. Covered now, Carlisle looked up to find Tyler standing there staring at her, his eyes strangely alive.

"You're very beautiful," he said in a husky voice, then he continued moving about the cabin, gathering any scraps of wood that could be used to fuel the fire.

She felt oddly aroused by the realization that Tyler had not been able to keep his eyes off her. She was surprised to discover she did not feel the least embarrassed. In fact, she was pleased he enjoyed her body as she did his, for he was a magnificently built man. Carlisle knew from experience there was not one ounce of excess flesh on the man. He was all muscle, lean and hard. Tyler had once confessed to her that he couldn't keep his hands off her. She knew the feeling herself. She enjoyed touching him. No, more than that, she *needed* to touch him.

Giving herself a good shake, Carlisle scooted her bottom along the floor of the cabin until she had the blanket secured sarong-style under her arms. "I-I'll do that," she winced, putting a hand out to stop him as Tyler picked up her wet clothes and proceeded to spread them over the rope to dry. Somehow it seemed such an intimate thing for him to do and there were times when intimacy was painful for her.

Tyler grabbed the first-aid kit and knelt at her feet, his jeans making that peculiar swishing sound that wet jeans make. He opened the lid of the kit and removed a Spandex bandage. "Let's start with your foot," he commented, deftly wrapping the width of material around her foot and ankle.

"Do you do this kind of thing often?" Carlisle inquired sardonically, as he quickly finished the job.

"Listen, honey, when you live out here away from the convenience of doctors, you get pretty self-sufficient. You'd be surprised at some of the things I've done."

She raised her brows quizzically. "I'll bet I would."

"Okay, let's see your hands next," Tyler instructed, withdrawing a bottle of antiseptic and a sealed surgical wipe from the box. Carlisle held her hands out palms up as she had been told. He gently washed the bits of dirt and stone from the abrasions. How odd that such strong calloused hands could treat her with such gentleness. "Does that hurt?" he asked.

She shook her head from side to side. "It stings a little, but that's all."

"This will definitely sting," he warned, uncorking the vial of antiseptic, "but we have to make sure those cuts don't get infected."

As he reached out to administer the first application Carlisle jerked her hands back against her chest. "Aren't you going to do what my mother always did when I scraped a knee or an elbow as a child?"

Tyler permitted himself a small sigh. "All right, I'll bite—what was it your mother always did?"

"Blow—you're supposed to blow on the cut when you put that stuff on. That way it doesn't sting as badly." She couldn't believe he was unfamiliar with this basic medical practice.

Tyler looked at her skeptically. "Blow?" He was incredulous.

"Yes, blow—the harder the better," she replied, preparing herself by taking a deep breath.

"Do we synchronize our watches, too?" he asked with a dead-serious face.

"No—" The woman clicked her tongue as if he were being preposterous. "Just pucker up and get ready."

"All right . . ." He shrugged his shoulders. "Are you ready?"

Carlisle posed her body as if a gun were about to go off signaling the start of a race. "Ready!"

The next several minutes were spent with a great deal of blowing on both of their parts. Tyler managed to sterilize most of the cuts and scrapes amid all the inhaling and exhaling, but it was no small effort.

"Whew! I'm glad that's over," Carlisle exclaimed, her face bright red from exertion.

"You were very brave, Carly. Surely such bravery

139

deserves a reward." The man's eyes flickered with humor.

"A reward?" Her manner was cautious, her tone suspicious.

Tyler bent and claimed her lips, kissing her deeply, passionately, until her head was filled with a darkness that threatened to engulf her.

"I'd rather have something to eat," she blurted out as Tyler pulled back. "I'm famished!"

He put his head back and laughed. "Flattery will get you nowhere with me, my dear."

"Oh, I didn't mean it like that." Carlisle rushed to make amends. "It's just that all I've had to eat since breakfast is half an apple and a little lukewarm iced tea." Her grimace was most eloquent.

"In that case, let's see what kind of sandwiches Rosemary packed, shall we?" He handed her one of the wrapped packets.

"Roast beef," she said without enthusiasm.

"Ham and cheese," he announced tentatively.

Then, as if some kind of unspoken negotiations had taken place between them, they exchanged sandwiches to their mutual satisfaction.

Tyler poured a cup of coffee from the thermos and offered it to Carlisle. "We'll have to share the cup. I hope you don't mind."

"Why, that's a silly question considering that you and I are—are stranded out here," she finished with a rush. She watched the man wolf down two sandwiches in quick succession. "Anyone would think you were the one who hadn't eaten all day."

Tyler glanced up unconcerned. "I discovered you were missing *before* I had dinner."

Carlisle felt duly chastised. "Oh—I'm sorry."

He broke into a broad grin. "That's okay. I ate a sandwich in the truck on the way up here."

"Tyler!" She tossed the cellophane wrapper at him in retaliation.

The man adeptly caught it in his fist and went on as if nothing had happened. "Would you like another sandwich? Rosemary packed enough for an army."

"No, thanks. Well, maybe just one more. Is there another ham and cheese in there?" When this sandwich was finally eaten too, Carlisle sat back satiated.

"How about a cigarette?" he offered. She nodded, watching him put it between his own lips before lighting it. Then he handed the cigarette to her. It was still warm from his mouth. "Now—why don't you tell me what possessed you to come all the way up here today?" It was a question he had been wanting to ask her from the first moment he had spotted the Jeep.

"It seemed like a good idea at the time." She sighed. "You were going to be busy all day with the cattle and Rosemary had gone shopping. I had seen so little of the area that I decided to do some sightseeing. I remembered George Henson mentioning Elizabethtown and Maria gave me the directions."

A tense frown bracketed the man's lips. "Weren't you aware of the storm warning that was out?"

"Not until I got caught in the middle of it," Carlisle ground through her teeth.

"Well, it doesn't matter now, anyway." Tyler carefully

141

skirted the argument he sensed brewing. "The storm should blow over by morning and we can head back to Chula Vista then."

She looked at him for a minute. "I'm sorry if I caused you a lot of trouble, Tyler."

"That's okay. I'm kind of getting used to it." He got to his feet and moved the stack of scrap wood he had salvaged to one side of the fireplace. "That should see us through the night," he commented, his conversation suddenly at a minimum. The man spread his poncho next to Carlisle's yet at a safe distance from the fire and covered it with the other blanket. "How about trying to get some sleep now?" His eyes evaded hers.

Carlisle realized she was beginning to feel warm again and dry, except for her hair. She fanned it out around her shoulders to catch the fire's drying warmth. She looked at Tyler out of the corner of her eye. He hadn't said one word of complaint, but his own clothes appeared to be soaked through. "Aren't you going to take off those wet things?" she said so softly her words seemed drowned out by the rain drumming on the roof of the cabin.

But Tyler must have heard her for he straightened up and undid the belt buckle at his waist. He pulled his shirt free and eased it off his chest, his skin glistening in the firelight. He removed his boots and jeans in unhurried movements; the rest of his clothes followed. He hung them over the makeshift clothesline next to hers.

"My shirt is practically dry," he said, handing it to her.

Carlisle slipped her arms into the sleeves and pulled the shirt around her. "Would you please help me stand up?" she asked, with a brittle sort of calm. Balancing on

142

one leg, she removed the blanket and held it out to him. "Here—you take this."

"Thanks, I think we're both going to need it," he acknowledged, with a perfunctory nod of his head. "Come on, honey, stretch out here." Tyler helped her onto the bed he had prepared for them, though it was no more than a blanket on a hard wooden floor.

Carlisle put her head down and tried to curl up into a ball, Tyler's shirt barely providing a modest covering—not that they weren't beyond modesty at this point. She felt him stretch out behind her, pulling the blanket over them both. He put an arm around her waist, using the other as a pillow for her head, but he made no further move to touch her.

His bare flesh burned her through the shirt, until her breath caught in her lungs. She lay there for some time, too tense, too aware of him to sleep. Then Carlisle could tell by his even breathing that Tyler had drifted off to sleep. Her eyes grew heavy and she joined him at last.

She roused some time during the night as Tyler got up to add wood to the fire. He went down on his haunches, stirring the hot coals until they burst anew into a bright flame, and remained there motionless for a minute or two. Then he turned and found Carlisle watching him as he had watched her earlier. With the fire tended to, Tyler stood up and came to her.

"It will keep us warmer if we stay together," she murmured, nuzzling her face into the side of his neck.

"It's the first law of survival," Tyler muttered thickly, pulling Carlisle to him.

His kiss was slow and tantalizing, licking at her mouth like the flames of a fire. It warmed her inside and out. His hands remained at her waist, the shirt clutched between his fingers as if to touch her was to get burned.

Carlisle snuggled closer, careful to keep her injured foot out of the way. It hadn't been giving her too much trouble and she was not about to do something foolish now.

Tyler buried his face in the mass of damp auburn hair that covered her shoulders. "I love you, Carly. God, I was worried out of my mind when we discovered you were missing!"

A shiver of excitement ran through her. "How did you know where to find me?"

He tightened his arms around her. "It wasn't easy. When I got back to the house Rosemary had no idea where you had gone. She mentioned Maria had been there as she left to do her shopping, so I called the Chavez place. I finally got it out of Maria that you had talked about coming up here to E-town. What the hell possessed you? I left word you were to stay put. I knew those dark clouds meant trouble," he said with a bitter emphasis.

"But Maria said . . ." Carlisle clamped her mouth shut.

Tyler spoke without looking at her. "What did Maria say?"

She swallowed heavily. "She . . . ah . . . said something about locoweed."

"Yes, a dozen head of cattle got into a patch." He crooked a suspicious brow in her direction. "Exactly what did little Miss Chavez say to you?'' He was not a man to be easily deterred.

Carlisle dismissed the subject with a wave of her hand. She lightly traced her lips along the line of his jaw, observing how it relaxed under her ministrations. "Let's not talk about Maria Chavez now, not tonight," she murmured, in her best sultry voice.

The man's eyes glinted steel. "Did you have some other topic of conversation in mind?"

She danced her fingers across the muscled wall of his chest in a way that could not possibly be misinterpreted. "No . . ." she confessed.

Tyler looked to heaven for patience. "If I keep kissing you, Carlisle, it's not going to end there—you know that as well as I do. You've had a tough time of it today. Your hands are all cut up and you have a bad ankle—"

Carlisle cut in abruptly. "If I'm not complaining, why should you?"

"I just don't want to do anything to hurt you," he murmured, his resolve weakening.

"You won't," she assured him, meeting his mouth as it came down on hers in a tender kiss.

While the storm began to subside outside the cabin walls, it only began anew inside. Tenderness evolved into passionate need as they explored all the ways their lips could satisfy each other.

His tongue teased the tip of her ear in a lazy circle, sending shivers rippling down her spine. Caressing hands left her waist to roam beneath the shirt he had given her, seeking and finding each vulnerable pulse point. When Tyler's fingers encountered the twin mounds of flesh, a moan broke from Carlisle's lips. Driven on by her response, he caught the budding nub between thumb and finger and gently molded it into an aroused peak.

Growing impatient with the barrier that separated them, the man made a sensuous production of undoing each button of the shirt in turn, kissing the length of skin exposed until he reached the golden expanse of her belly. His hand moved along her thigh and back up the other side.

"Your shirt is going to get all wrinkled," Carlisle mumbled, wiggling free of his embrace long enough to remove it. Tyler gave the shirt a toss, not even bothering to look to see where it landed.

"Carlisle . . ." A moan issued forth from his lips as he coaxed hers to open to him.

She ran her fingers into his hair and down the back of his neck. Tyler's skin was soft to the touch, his hair thick and fine. Seemingly enchanted, her hands moved in a caress over his shoulders, broad and full of the promise of strength as they were. With her little finger she twisted french knots in the mass of hair on his chest, beguiled by its rich silky texture.

The man's lips trailed along Carlisle's arm from wrist to shoulder, alerting every nerve ending to his feather-light caress and its consequences. "Oh, Carly, if you only knew what you do to me!" Tyler exhaled in a rush of warm sweet breath that was as intoxicating as any wine.

In her thirst she reached for his mouth with her own, plummeting deeper and deeper into the vortex of their mutually fed desire. He could arouse such a need in her that it nearly frightened her with its intensity. Yet she rushed to meet his passion—fear a flimsy thing beside her love for this man. "Tyler!" In that one word she expressed all the love in her heart, all the hunger in her body for his.

The man cupped her face in his hands and looked down into her eyes with undisguised passion. "I want to make love to you, sweetheart. You know that, don't you?" He leaned over her, softly parting her lips with his.

Carlisle had no other answer but the wild leap her heart took beneath his hand and the eager participation of her mouth moving furiously against his. In a repetition that somehow seemed new each time, he lowered his head to savor other delicacies. His tongue made darting forays from one ripe nipple to the other. She grasped his hips between her hands, anchoring herself to the solid weight of his body.

The woman twisted her head from side to side, little cries of discovery bubbling to the surface. She arched toward the man, seeking the fulfillment promised by his flesh on hers. He probed deeper and deeper until he became her whole world.

Then Tyler tore his mouth away from hers and took her hands in his. He raised them to his lips, tenderly pressing a kiss to each angry red slash that marred her skin. Seeking to cushion the woman from the hard cabin floor, he rolled over and carefully pulled her onto his chest.

They were a matched set. Her long legs stretched out along his muscular ones, her hips fitted to his flesh, her full breasts flattened against the agitated rise and fall of his chest. Their hands eagerly explored the other's body from thigh to shoulder until they both knew they had reached the point of no return.

"You are the woman I have always needed, Carly," Tyler confessed against her mouth. "The woman I never dared dream of having."

Carlisle's whole body shook, her skin oddly damp. She raised her head and there was a world of emotion in her eyes as they gazed into his. "I never dreamed about having a man like you, Tyler. I never knew there was a man like you."

Then there were no more playful caresses meant to drive the other to the brink of need, no more teasing, as they wordlessly agreed the moment had come to find the mutual fulfillment they could only find through each other. The storm outside was forgotten as a greater storm burned and raged within the four walls of the rustic cabin. But that, too, was forgotten—all was forgotten in the ecstasy of their love.

8

Hm . . . Tyler . . ." Carlisle mumbled as she rolled over and instinctively reached out for him. "Tyler?" She was awake now and knew that he was gone from her side.

She struggled to a sitting position, hampered by the blanket wrapped tightly about her like a cocoon. She was alone in the cabin. She sensed it before her eyes told her it was true. She twisted free of the encumbrance and slowly got to her feet, every bone and muscle of her body protesting against the slightest movement.

The shirt Tyler had literally given her off his back the night before lay in a crumpled heap beside her. She clutched it to her breasts and stared at the empty room. Her clothes were still there, draped over the length of rope he had rigged up, but his jeans were missing. The cowboy boots were gone from the spot by the fireplace where he had placed them to dry.

In her bare feet, Carlisle limped over to her clothes. She pulled them down and began to dress, despite the fact that they were still quite damp.

"Ugh!" She grimaced. Even her socks were cold and clammy against her skin. There was nothing to be done but to put them on and get back to Chula Vista as quickly as possible. She struggled into her jump suit, shuddering as the damp material stuck to her body.

Once she was dressed, she hobbled about the cabin, shaking out blankets and ponchos and neatly folding them in a pile by the door. She took the rope down and stood back to survey the room. In the revealing light of morning that seeped in through a crack in the shutters, it was only a dusty old ramshackle cabin. Nevertheless, Carlisle knew a moment of regret. She had been strangely happy here for a few hours and she doubted that she would ever return.

The warmth and passion of the night spent in Tyler's arms faded in the harsh unrelenting light of day. Carlisle felt lousy, and even without a mirror to tell her so, she knew she looked bedraggled as well. There was no brush to soften the mass of auburn tangles, no warm bubble bath to wash away the dirt and grime.

She was nibbling on a tasteless sandwich, washing it down with a cup of cold coffee, when Tyler suddenly appeared in the doorway. There was the telltale shadow of a beard on his chin. His chest was bare and streaked with an odd mixture of mud and grease. Yet in spite of it all, Carlisle felt the breath propelled back into her lungs at the sight of the man. Would it always be this way each time he walked into a room?

"G-good morning," she stammered as he stood there, silent and unapproachable. "You'll be needing your shirt now, won't you? Thank you for letting me use it." She was chattering nervously, handing the shirt to him with some reluctance, as if it somehow symbolized the end of the intimacy they had shared in this very cabin.

Carlisle wanted to rush into his arms and say good morning properly, but the magic was gone. This man with the tight thin line for a mouth and dark stern eyes was virtually a stranger, not the tender lover she had known a few short hours ago. He stood there preoccupied, out of her reach. She felt suddenly that she existed in a universe occupied only by her own heartbeats.

The man finally deemed it necessary to speak. "I checked out your Jeep this morning. It seems to be running all right." The explanation came as he pulled on the crumpled shirt. "I honestly couldn't say why it wouldn't start for you last night."

"Perhaps something got wet that shouldn't. It came down in buckets for a while," Carlisle suggested rather feebly.

"Could be." Tyler grunted, crouching by the fireplace to see if the ashes were cold. With that done to his apparent satisfaction, he uncoiled his lean frame and turned to her. "It's been one hell of a night. Let's get going."

She could only nod her head. It had not all been hellish, she thought, picking up the thermos. There had been a bit of heaven here, too.

"It seems more like a dream now," Carlisle murmured

pensively as they picked their way back down the hillside. The going was slippery and muddy, but the morning was fresh and clear—the calm that so often comes after a storm.

"I'm surprised you didn't say 'nightmare,'" Tyler interjected as he stowed the supplies in the pickup.

The woman stood for a moment absorbing the peacefulness that reigned all around them. "No, not a nightmare." She paused thoughtfully. "Never that." She glanced up at the man only to discover he was watching her with an intensity, an anger that was almost frightening.

"You could have been seriously hurt, Carlisle. Storms in these mountains are a danger to be respected. You don't go gallivanting off as though you were on your way to a picnic. You scared the hell out of Rosemary and me by disappearing like that! I hope you've learned your lesson." His hold on her arm finally relaxed. "It may be treacherous until we get back to the main road. Follow exactly where I lead," he ordered in a cryptic tone, "and for God's sake—drive carefully!" Tyler slammed the door of the Jeep shut behind her and took off for the pickup with a purposeful gait.

If Carlisle had thought the drive up to Elizabethtown the previous day was arduous and exhausting, it was nothing compared to the long slow trek back out of the mountains. Her mind and body were numb with fatigue. There was a great throbbing behind her eyes that made concentration impossible. Her head bounced and flopped on her neck like a newborn baby's. It was only through sheer desperation and willpower that she was even able to keep the Jeep on the road. By the time they reached Chula Vista, she was feeling strangely feverish. She turned off the engine and sat there staring straight ahead, her eyes unseeing.

Tyler jerked the door of the Jeep open and half-carried half-dragged her toward the house. Rosemary Quinn came running to meet them, her apron flapping in the breeze.

"Thank the Lord, you're both all right!" she exclaimed. "We've all been worried sick." She held the kitchen door ajar and followed them into the house.

"We've had a pretty rotten time of it," Tyler stated tersely and rather unnecessarily, dumping Carlisle on the nearest chair.

"I'll take her right upstairs and run a tub of hot water." Rosemary Quinn was immediately all efficiency. "Oh, dear—what have you done to yourself?" She gasped, catching sight of the younger woman's hands and the bandage prominently displayed on her ankle.

"She fell down a mountain," the man answered for her, seemingly unaware of the exaggeration. "She's also tired and hungry," he added, as an afterthought. "Make sure she has something to eat, will you, Rosemary?" He spoke as if he were washing his hands of the whole affair and none too soon either.

"I'll take care of everything, Tyler. You'd better see to yourself."

"I'm all right, Rosemary." He waved his hand dismissively. "Or at least I will be."

"Running off last night into that storm . . . and without your supper," she muttered, helping Carlisle to her feet.

"Tyler . . ." Carlisle finally found her voice, weak though it was. She looked up into his face, her eyes sending him an urgent message. He must know she needed some word, some sign of reassurance from him now to restore her shattered confidence in their love.

But it was not to be. The man responded with a tense frown, his brows drawing together. "Go along with Rosemary. She'll see to everything you need," he said through his teeth. "I have some things to take care of that can't wait." Tyler abruptly swung on his heel and left the two women to their own devices without any further explanation.

She was obviously not one of those things, Carlisle lamented to herself as the housekeeper helped her up the stairs to her room.

"You sit right there while I draw your bath," Rosemary said in a gentle tone as she settled her charge on the edge of the bed. She gave the young woman's hand an understanding pat. Such a small gesture, yet it brought a flood of tears rushing to Carlisle's eyes. "There, there, my dear. You've been through a harrowing experience, but we'll have you feeling better in no time."

"I-I know . . ." Carlisle nodded and accepted the tissue handed her. She sat motionless, listening to the comforting sounds of the housekeeper as she moved about the bathroom. The influx of hot water into the tub sent a haze of steam billowing into the bedroom. Yet none of it really registered in her confused state of mind.

"Here—let me help you," Rosemary murmured, as if she were speaking to a child.

Carlisle got to her feet and allowed herself to be undressed. A robe was gently wrapped about her shoulders as she was guided into the adjoining bathroom.

"Do you think you could manage on your own for a

few minutes?" Rosemary asked, hovering tentatively at her side.

Carlisle momentarily shook off the inertia that had held her in its grip and bestowed a smile on the woman that was more bravado than confidence. "Y-yes, of course . . . thank you, Rosemary."

"You just soak until I return." The housekeeper's words floated back to her as she whisked out the door.

Carlisle stood there a moment or two longer, then dropped the bathrobe to the tiled floor and gingerly stepped into the tub of fragrant water, intending to do exactly as she had been instructed. She stretched out her long lithe frame and put her head back with an exaggerated sigh. The movement of the water rippling over her body in soothing waves was a delicious mesmerizing luxury. She could feel the tension ease all the way from the cord in her neck down to her swollen ankle as the warmth enveloped her.

It may have taken no more than a few minutes in a hot bath to ease the soreness from her bones and muscles, but the woman's emotions were still in a turmoil, running the gamut from joy to despair. She lay there, eyes closed, trying desperately to reconcile in her own mind the loving man of the previous night with the stern, disapproving stranger she had encountered this morning.

Carlisle was well aware that Tyler was angry with her and she was quite certain she knew why. Going off without a word as she had done and then heading into a potentially dangerous situation, both to herself and to him, was unforgivably stupid! And to think she had been fool enough to trust Maria Chavez, when any amount of common sense would have dictated otherwise. She shook her head disgustedly. That had been stupid as well. People simply did not change overnight. How many times would she have to learn that the hard way before she caught on?

With the seed of doubt planted in her mind like a malignant growth, Carlisle shuddered at the implications of her naïveté. Perhaps Tyler's rather "timely" declaration of love had in reality been no more or less than physical desire speaking. He certainly seemed to be having second thoughts about it now.

Come to think of it, there had never been any mention of a future together, no discussion of marriage beyond a natural curiosity as to why she wasn't already in a state of wedded bliss at the age of twenty-nine. Carlisle admitted all this to herself and more, with a ruthlessness that would leave no false hopes intact.

No, it had always been "I need you," "I want you," "I desire you." And Tyler Carson would not be the first man to use those little words a woman wants to hear to his own advantage. Oh, dear God—what if a summer affair was all he had ever wanted from her?

Carlisle forced her heart to retreat from her throat, where it had lodged like a bitter pill. Perhaps she had toyed briefly with the idea of a love affair with Tyler, but she had just as quickly recognized that this was the one man she could not walk away from unscathed. She knew that for the rest of her life he would be the man against whom all other men would be measured and found wanting. To leave him now would be condemning some vital part of her to an early death—it would shrivel up and become a hard cold stone where a loving heart should be.

For Carlisle Scott was a woman who had always strived for and obtained only the best. How could she settle someday for second best when it came to love?

She wanted to scream her outrage, cry out her pain and frustration. Tyler had ruined her emotionally and physically for any other man. No matter who came into her life in the years ahead, it would be *his* laugh, *his* kiss, *his* lovemaking that would remain imprinted on her soul. Oh, Lord! she cried from the depths of her being. She was such a bloody fool to have rushed into an affair like some naïve trusting eighteen-year-old.

When the tears came—as they finally did—they were bitter, not self-pitying. And when she at last raised her head, Carlisle felt as if she had aged a hundred years in the space of a few minutes. She would never be quite the same woman again.

God, she was tired! Far beyond the physical, she was tired in mind and spirit. She must have dozed off, for she did not hear the housekeeper return until a soft knock came at the bathroom door.

"Carlisle—it's Rosemary."

"Come in," she called out sleepily, slipping further beneath the camouflage of soapy bubbles.

"Would you like me to wash your hair for you?" inquired the same gentle voice.

"Oh, Rosemary, I couldn't ask you to do that," Carlisle protested without vigor.

"Now, now, I wouldn't be doing any more than your own mother would want to do if she were here," the woman crooned. "We're none of us too old for a little mothering every now and then."

"I-I know, but . . ."

"I have a daughter about your age. Did I ever tell you that?" Rosemary chattered as she proceeded to pour a pitcher of warm water over Carlisle's head and added a dab of shampoo. "Caroline is married to a fine man. They live in Minneapolis and have two young children—a boy and a girl. Freddie is six now and Lisa is four." She sighed, working the lather through the long auburn tresses. "Of course, I don't get to see them as often as I'd like to."

Carlisle drew a breath and spoke slowly. "You must miss them."

"I do," the woman admitted. "I suppose that's why I tend to mother Tyler—although what he needs, in my opinion, is a good woman by his side." The housekeeper drew a fresh pitcher of water from the basin and began to rinse the shampoo from Carlisle's hair. "Why hasn't a beautiful young woman like you gotten married?" The transition was not very subtle, but then Rosemary Quinn's transitions never were. She was a country woman, outspoken and candid.

"I suppose I've never met the—ah . . . right man," the younger woman mumbled, nearly adding "until now."

"Well, I don't know what's wrong with the men today if they let someone like you slip through their fingers. I do declare," Rosemary muttered, shaking her head. "Now, now, don't start to cry again, honey." She held out a big bath sheet as Carlisle stepped from the tub.

"I'm not usually so weepy." Carlisle laughed, through her tears. "I guess this whole business has gotten to me more than I realized."

A knowing smile softened the other woman's features into a benign expression. "Into bed with you this minute,

158

young lady!" she bullied, once she managed to slip a nightgown over Carlisle's head. She took a dry towel to the tendrils of wet hair and vigorously rubbed until every nerve ending was atingle. She even insisted on combing out the freshly washed mass herself.

"You're spoiling me something awful," Carlisle murmured, purring like a kitten.

"None of us are too old for . . ."

". . . for a little spoiling," she finished for her.

"I'm off to the kitchen now. I left Tyler with a big bowl of homemade vegetable soup and I want to be certain he's left some for you. I'll bring you up a nice tray and then I think a few hours of sleep would be in order." Rosemary stood up and straightened her rumpled apron.

"Thank you for everything, Rosemary." Carlisle's head involuntarily dropped back on the pillows.

"You've got an awful lot of color in those cheeks," the housekeeper noted, turning back to her self-appointed charge. A cool hand was placed on her forehead. "I believe I'll get you a couple of aspirin before I go," she stated with a scowl.

Carlisle had her aspirin and the hot soup, although in her current condition she could not do the latter justice. The last thing she remembered was Rosemary Quinn closing the shades at the windows, plunging the bedroom into twilight.

The clock on the bedside table informed Carlisle she had slept nearly two hours when she once again awakened. She knew immediately that her fever was gone. The insistent growling in her stomach told her she could do that soup justice now. Not about to take advantage of Rosemary any more than she already had, she got out of bed under her own power and pulled the robe on over her nightgown. She felt a little light-headed, but was determined to make it to the kitchen under her own power this time.

She had reached the top of the staircase when voices directly below her in the entranceway caused her to freeze in her tracks. She could neither advance nor retreat without giving herself away, and so she remained posed at the top of the stairs. One hand clutched the banister in an effort to steady herself. She choked back the telling gasp that would have revealed her presence to those below. For there in the front hall was a smiling, seductive Maria Chavez, looking anything *but* the contrite child of yesterday. And there, too, was a smiling and equally eager Tyler Carson welcoming her!

"Niña—I can't tell you how pleased I am that you could come over." The deep baritone resounded in a verbal caress that made Carlisle wince. How many times had she responded to that same seductive quality in his voice? "I must confess you are looking very beautiful and very grown up, Maria," the man continued, in the same vein.

The girl was quite obviously thrilled to find that Tyler's attitude toward her had finally changed. "I was hoping you would call, amado, and you did, of course." Maria's laugh was deliberately pitched low, emphasizing the intimacy of their conversation.

She raised her face for Tyler's customary kiss upon greeting, but this was not the brotherly peck on the forehead or cheek Carlisle had previously seen him bestow on the dark young beauty. No, indeed, this was a warm lingering union of their lips that left Maria flushed with pleasure. It was a kiss such as a man gives a woman who has caught his fancy. And Maria Chavez responded with all the passion stored up inside her for this man.

Carlisle desperately wanted to run away. She couldn't bear to stand there and watch this scene played to its natural conclusion. But her feet refused to cooperate.

"I must say, darling, you look none the worse for your wild-goose chase." The girl gave a smothered laugh as she traced the line of Tyler's jaw with a brightly painted fingernail. "We've all heard about Miss Scott's escapade yesterday, of course. I wonder whatever possessed the woman to take off like that?" Carlisle marveled at the innocent expression Maria managed as she gazed up into the man's face. "Funny—Miss Scott *seemed* like a fairly intelligent creature. Oh, who understands these gringos?" Then she laughed again, louder and longer.

Tyler responded by slipping an arm about Maria's shoulders and drawing her to his side. His head was bent toward the bright young face as if he were about to claim her lips in another kiss. "You would never do anything so stupid, would you, my dear?"

"How could I?" she boasted. "I know this entire area like the back of my hand."

"Would you like to join me in a glass of wine, niña?" the man murmured in her ear.

The girl laughed with a laughter born of pleasure and power and a feeling of triumph. "I would love to," she answered rather breathlessly.

Tyler's arm visibly tightened around the slender frame. "I think it's time we discussed your future plans, don't you?" He paused significantly, as they strolled like lovers into the living room. Their voices grew even lower and

161

more initmate until the woman eavesdropping from above could not make out a single word of what they said.

Fatigue and strain had shorn Carlisle of her defenses. The tears welled from her eyes and ran unheeded down her cheeks. She was nearly doubled over as wave after wave of nausea and humiliation washed over her. She felt like someone had punched her in the stomach. Stuffing her fist in her mouth to stifle the cry that threatened to rise to the surface, she blindly stumbled down the hallway and into her bedroom, closing the door behind her.

"Oh, God—no!" she groaned as she shook her head from side to side. She leaned back against the door, letting it absorb some of the weakness that seemed to have invaded every bone of her body. "You fool!" she hissed in self-deprecation. "You actually believed he loved you. You believed every lousy fairy tale he spun!" And Maria Chavez—the child had been clever, deviously so. She had been outwitted by a girl of seventeen!

Carlisle sunk to her knees beside the bed, pounding the mattress with her fist. The tears came again, hot and stinging, burning her cheeks like molten lava. Cheeks sensitized by the stubble of Tyler's beard as he had sworn his love last night in the mountain cabin. But that had happened long ago and to someone else.

When her tears had momentarily spent themselves, Carlisle slowly got to her feet and fumbled along the top of the dresser until she found an open pack of cigarettes. She shook one free and lit it without thought. She took two deep draws before crushing it in an ashtray and lighting a second.

Then the agony she had felt as she unwillingly witnessed the scene between Tyler and Maria struck anew like a rapier thrust to the heart. Carlisle squeezed her eyes tightly shut until they were no more than two slits in her face. She refused to give in to tears again so soon.

Tyler did not love her. That awful truth had to be faced at last. Oh, he had no doubt desired her in bed as a temporary sexual diversion—but he didn't love her. Carlisle couldn't even bring herself to blame Maria Chavez at this point. The poor child's only mistake was that she too loved Tyler. He was the one who should carry the full burden of blame. A man did not look elsewhere if he shared the same feelings for a woman that she felt for him. And to think that *she* had loved Tyler with all she was capable of giving while he had blithely taken her offering as a momentary satisfaction for his male appetites!

"Damn you, Tyler Carson!" She ground her teeth. Pain twisted around inside her and came out as anger— pure and awful in its intensity. Dammit all, where was her pride? she demanded of herself.

Crushing the second unsmoked cigarette in the ashtray, Carlisle Scott regally drew herself up to her full five feet seven inches of height and thrust out her chin in a gesture of determination. When nothing else remained, she could always count on her fierce personal pride to come to the rescue.

She immediately went into action—her only thought to get away from Tyler and Chula Vista and New Mexico as quickly as possible. She pulled her suitcases from the closet and lugged them one by one across the room to the bed. She unlatched each piece and threw it open, then turned to the dresser drawers. Grabbing a handful of lacy underthings and nightgowns, Carlisle stuffed them into one of the smaller cases.

She had the drawers emptied and was headed for the closet when a feeling of dizziness overtook her. Once the worst of it had passed, she made her way to the bathroom and drank a few sips of cool water. Then she returned to her task with renewed vigor.

By God, she would not spend one more night in that man's house! He would just have to find himself some other fool to finish his precious dam. For the first time in an otherwise unblemished career, Carlisle was walking off a job before it was completed. She was a woman first and then an engineer, and the woman's emotions were ruling supreme.

She clenched an armful of dresses and pants from the closet and began to rip them free of their hangers, tossing one and all into the larger bag, unmindful of wrinkles—unmindful of everything but the need to get away from this house as soon as she could. So intent was she on her task that her brain scarcely registered the soft rap at the bedroom door.

"Carly?"

It was the one voice she had hoped not to hear. She paused but said nothing. Then she went on with her packing, though packing was perhaps not an accurate description of what she was doing.

"Carlisle, are you awake?" Tyler persisted, apparently not put off by her failure to reply. He knocked again—a knock not to be ignored.

"G-go away!" she choked, angry with herself for the trembling in her voice, the tears that blurred her vision.

164

She thought of bolting the lock—but too late. The door flew open, swinging back and forth on its hinges from the force of the blow. She looked up unwillingly to where Tyler stood framed in the doorway.

In one sweeping glance, the man took in the disheveled scene before him—Carlisle's distraught appearance, the red-rimmed hazel eyes, the unnatural color of her cheeks, the clothes strewn across the bed, the open drawers and suitcases.

He advanced into the room with the bold undaunted gait of the cowboy. "What in the hell do you think you're doing?" he demanded, in a voice of thunder.

Carlisle's answer was succinct. "I'm packing," she said, voice and manner dry.

The man uttered an impatient sound as he grasped her hands in an attempt to halt their frenzied activity. "I can see that. The question is *why.*" He raised his eyebrows expressively.

She turned to stone, refusing to meet his dark questioning gaze. "I really don't see that it's any of your business." She sniffed, with regal disdain. "Now will you please let go of my arm?"

Tyler took his hands back, but refused to retreat. "None of my business?" He slowly released his breath as if he were mentally counting to ten. "All right, what kind of game are you playing, Carly?"

"I never play games. I'm leaving, Tyler." Carlisle made certain he understood there was to be no discussion on that point. She made another trip to the closet to collect a second armload of clothes.

The man's hand went to the cord at the back of his neck, rubbing it in an absent motion. "Would it be asking too much to know what brought this on?" He gestured impatiently toward the jumble of clothing and baggage.

"I don't care to discuss it with you," she stated sharply, an unmistakable note of bitterness creeping into her voice.

"You don't care to discuss it with me?" The tight rein on his temper slipped. "You sure as hell will discuss it with me!" he roared, grabbing the dress she was folding and tossing it aside.

They glared at each other over the open lid of her suitcase. The lines of the battle were drawn.

"A show of brute force, Tyler? Is that all you 'cowboys' know?" Carlisle made certain it was an insult.

The man's eyes narrowed dangerously in his face. "Maybe a little 'brute force,' as you call it, would get through to you, 'honey.'" The latter was anything but an endearment. "I can see I've been far too patient and understanding with you all along. I made a mistake in thinking you were somehow different than other women, in approaching you as a mature, intelligent adult. But it's still not too late to show you who's boss." He took a menacing step toward her.

Carlisle's eyes went wide with a primitive fear. She had an odd and rather unpleasant feeling in the pit of her stomach. "Don't you dare put a hand on me, Tyler Carson!" She bit off each word. "So help me God, if you lay so much as a finger on me I'll never speak to you again."

"That sounds like a dare to me." Tyler grinned savagely, like a cat playing with a mouse it knows it has cornered. "Never dare a 'middle-aged' cowboy, sweetheart." There was an implied threat in his tone.

The woman took a deep shuddering breath and straightened her shoulders. "I am trying very hard to keep this conversation on an adult level," she enunciated clearly.

"Then where do you think you're going, you little fool?" he hissed.

"I told you. I'm leaving. I'm going back to Denver this evening," she finally admitted.

Tyler looked at her as though he would quite gladly like to strangle her. "There aren't any planes to Denver at this time of day," he scoffed. "That's the stupidest thing you've ever come up with!"

"Oh, yes, I am fully aware of your opinion of my intelligence," she cried out derisively.

"And just what is that supposed to mean?" The man swung back and forth like a pendulum between anger and confusion. He definitely preferred to be in control of any situation he found himself in and he was definitely *not* in control now. It filled him with emotions he could not easily sort out.

"Why don't you ask Maria Chavez? You two seem pretty chummy." Carlisle hated herself for saying the words, but they seemed to pop out without permission. She knew she sounded like a jealous shrew.

"What the hell does Maria have to do with all of this?" Tyler was utterly confused now.

"It doesn't matter." She clamped her mouth shut on the subject. "I am planning to leave here tonight and that's that. You'll just have to get yourself another engineer to finish your precious dam." Carlisle recognized in some detached part of herself that she was on the verge of hysteria for the first time in her life.

It seemed that Tyler had reached the end of his tether as well. He grabbed her by the shoulders, unaware that he shook her as he spoke. "You're being ridiculous, do you know that? You're crazy!" His face was devoid of color, his hands bruising to her flesh, strengthened as they were by his anger. "I want some straight answers from you, Carlisle, and I want them now!"

Her eyes widened with alarm. Her teeth clattered against each other in her head. "Tyler—Tyler, you're hurting me!" she repeated sharply.

The man quickly removed his hands and took a step backward, obviously still fighting some kind of battle within himself. "Lord, but you're an exasperating woman. I don't know if I want to strangle that pretty little neck of yours or make love to you!" he rasped in barely controlled fury.

"One is as preferable to me as the other," she hissed, lacing her voice with contempt.

An indefinable expression flitted across Tyler's features; his jaw muscles twitched in an oddly nervous rhythm. "I can see that we're going to get absolutely nowhere with this conversation as long as you're intent on behaving like an hysterical female."

"I couldn't agree with you more—we're getting absolutely nowhere with this conversation," she repeated.

"Well, you can just put all of this back, sweetheart. You aren't going anywhere tonight." With a wide sweep of his hand, he indicated the whole wild disarray of clothes and suitcases. "You and I haven't finished our little chat yet—by a long shot. We will continue this discussion first thing in the morning, when hopefully you will have calmed down enough to make sense." He seized a handful of her things and ruthlessly stuffed them back into one of the open drawers.

"I prefer to do that myself." She sniffed indignantly.

"Then see that you do," he grated through his teeth as he turned toward the door. "And Carlisle—don't get any ideas about sneaking off in the middle of the night. There's no place you can run to that I won't be able to find you." It was not an idle threat, but a promise.

Carlisle had had it with this man—with all men, for that matter. "You can go to hell, Tyler Carson!" she called out defiantly.

With his hand on the doorknob, Tyler hesitated and then turned back halfway into the bedroom. "If I do, honey, I promise I'll take you with me." Then he was gone, leaving her alone in the tomblike silence of her room.

Carlisle clutched her hands in impotent rage. Damn the man! Didn't he realize he was tearing her in two? The twin forces of love and hate battled within her until she crumpled under the strain. She curled up in the big chair beside the bed, wrapping her arms about her knees and burying her face in their cold comfort.

It was some time before she lifted her head. She could not stay here; that was all there was to it. No matter what threats Tyler voiced, she had to leave Chula Vista and she must do so tonight.

With a strange sort of calmness, she rose to her feet. She dressed in a pair of slacks and a sweater and mechanically began the long process of packing all over again. She selected the bare essentials for her smallest bag, the only one she intended to take with her now. The others would have to be sent on after her departure.

Carlisle worked slowly and methodically until she stood back to survey the results. The bedroom looked as it had that first day—neat and tidy, with her luggage stacked in one corner. She considered leaving a note for Rosemary, but no viable explanation for her hasty departure was forthcoming. It was too personal and too complicated to explain in a letter, anyway.

Once every detail had been seen to, she switched off the lights and sat in the dark, smoking and trying not to think beyond this night. She nearly jumped when a knock came at the door.

"Carlisle, it's Rosemary."

Relief ran through her like quicksilver at the sound of the woman's voice. "Y-yes . . ."

"I've brought you a bedtime snack, dear. I-I thought you might be hungry. You didn't eat much earlier today."

Sobs choked in her throat, preventing her immediate reply. "That's very sweet of you," she finally murmured.

The housekeeper spoke softly, as if her lips were pressed close to the door. "Is there anything I can do to help?"

"No—no thank you, Rosemary," Carlisle said, her voice sinking almost to a whisper. "Would you mind just leaving the tray outside the door. I-I'll get it in a minute."

"All right, dear." She could hear the extended sigh in the woman's tone. "Good night, Carlisle."

"Good night, Rosemary . . . and good-bye," she added, for her own ears only.

Carlisle was grateful for that bedtime snack, realizing she needed something to give her the energy to execute the rest of her plans for that night. She forced herself to eat both sandwiches and drink the glass of milk, though the food seemed to stick in her throat.

With her course of action decided, she was anxious to be on her way. Thank goodness, ranchers retired early. She waited a full hour after the house had settled down before making any move. Then with her one small suitcase in hand, she stealthily made her way down the stairs and out the back door. Without so much as a backward glance, Carlisle Scott climbed into the Jeep and drove away.

"You either cry or drive, Carly; you can't do both!" She scolded herself, wiping the tears with the back of her hand. "Drive now—you can always cry later."

9

~~~~~~~~~~~~~~~~

Carlisle fit the key in the lock, turned it once to the left, and nudged the door of the motel room open with her foot.

Tyler was right about one thing, she admitted wearily, there weren't any flights from Santa Fe to Denver at this time of the night. She had booked a reservation on the first plane going out in the morning, however. Meanwhile, the only logical thing to do was to check into the motel nearest to the airport. She had accomplished this in the last five minutes.

Dropping her suitcase on the luggage rack by the bed, Carlisle strolled over to the air-conditioning unit and clicked the dial to ventilation only. She flipped the lid on a can of cola she had obtained from a machine just down the corridor from her room and sank into a chair, kicking her shoes off haphazardly in the process.

Tyler would be positively livid once he found she had jumped ship despite his explicit orders to the contrary! She was certain of that now in light of her recent discoveries about his personality. The man very definitely had a temper. She had seen that for herself this evening. As much as she tried to tell herself that she, too, would have been frustrated in his shoes, she had no intention of hanging around for his eloquent explanations.

Carlisle recognized how vulnerable she was when it came to Tyler Carson. And she had too much pride to submit to a man who had used her for his own physical gratification. That was the decisive point—she had too much pride to beg for love from any man. Yet her body seemed to have a mind of its own when it came to Tyler. She couldn't trust herself with him and so she had done the only thing she could for survival—she had run away. While running away from problems was not her usual style, Carlisle could not bring herself to condemn the action in this case. She desperately needed time to recover from the blow dealt her earlier this afternoon.

She got to her feet and puzzled for a moment whether it was worth changing into a nightgown for what was left of the night. She looked down at the casual slacks and sweater she wore. They were the only change of clothes she had brought with her, and unless she wished to show up in Denver tomorrow looking every bit as harried as she felt, she'd better not sleep in them tonight.

Carlisle quickly peeled the outfit from her body and hung it in the closet of the small room. Then she slipped into the one nightgown she had thought to throw in at the last minute. Propping herself up in the bed, she sipped absentmindedly at what was left of the cold drink.

And she had thought she was such a damned good judge of human character! If it didn't hurt so much to admit how wrong she had been, Carlisle was sure she would be laughing right now at her own foible. Yes—she knew her men all right—as well as any two-time loser would.

It had felt so right with Tyler—that's what hurt. She had honestly believed him when he said he loved her, more fool she. Yet she had to confess he had never made any commitments or promises for the future. She had simply been too blinded by her emotions to see where they were headed.

Face it, she had not expected to fall head over heels in love with the man either, a small inner voice whispered. No one ever expects to get burned when they enter a love affair, and yet it happens every day. She had always thought she was too intelligent, too cautious to get caught in that web. Well, she was good and truly caught this time. She was in love with an intelligent, attractive, charming *rat!*

Carlisle gave her pillow one good punch with her fist. What she felt now was anger and frustration and a certain puzzlement, but she knew in the weeks and months and years ahead, there would be time for regret as well. Regret for what she had almost had, for the love she could never forget.

She supposed it was like any traumatic loss; one went through a period of mourning, followed by anger, and then hopefully moved on to some kind of acceptance of what had happened.

But Lord, to always see him in a crowd, only to come closer and find it wasn't him. To hear a voice in the same deep baritone and glide toward it and know it could not be. To see bits and pieces of the man no matter where she went or what she did. The pain would come in small ways to tear at her heart, never quite letting it heal.

To lie in her bed in the dead of the night and dream of Tyler's mouth on hers, his hands performing their magic on her responsive body, his flesh smooth and stimulating against her flesh, only to wake and find herself alone. There was a certain cruelty that came with loving. The woman wasn't sure she believed it was better to have loved and lost than never to have loved at all. Would she have given up a single moment in Tyler's arms if she had suspected that this was how it would end? With her in a second-rate motel in Santa Fe, about to walk out of his life forever? Something told Carlisle no.

"Oh, Tyler . . ." She put her head down on the pillow and indulged in a moment or two of self-pity.

Then as if by simply saying his name, she had somehow conjured up the man himself, there was an unexpected pounding on the motel door. "Carlisle—I know you're in there!" came the familiar gruff voice. "We have to talk."

How could she possibly be happy to hear his voice? She must remember she was supposed to be furious with the man. Carlisle bounced off the bed and approached the door with caution. "I think we've said all we have to say to each other," she finally threw back at him.

"Maybe you have, lady, but I haven't," Tyler stated, in no uncertain terms. "Now we can either shout at each other through this door, in which case the entire neighborhood is going to know our business—or you can open it so we can behave like civilized adults."

Put like that, what choice did she have? Carlisle had no desire to be kicked out of this motel and be forced to spend the rest of the night sitting up in some uncomfortable chair at the airport. So she pulled the nightgown closer about her, having failed to include a bathrobe in her emergency supplies, and undid the chain lock and peeked around the crack in the door.

Tyler's face was masked by darkness. "Let me in, Carly—please." There was a slight edge to his voice.

"All right, but only because if I don't you'll wake up the entire motel with the racket you're making," she rationalized needlessly for both of their benefits, letting him in. "How did you know where to find me?" It was the first question to pop into her head.

"I knew you'd never get a flight out of Santa Fe tonight. I figured you would stay as close to the airport as you could, so I drove around until I saw the Jeep." He made it sound so simple.

"So much for sneaking off in the middle of the night," she mumbled sarcastically.

"You can't say I didn't warn you, honey. I made it clear if you ran away I would find you, regardless of where or when."

"And you are a man of your word, aren't you, Tyler?" She sneered with blatant skepticism.

The man came dangerously close, but made no move to touch her. "Sit down!" he ordered, indicating the chair she had recently vacated. "I think it's time you and I did some plain talking, Miss Carlisle Scott. None of this fancy mumbo jumbo, but good old-fashioned plain talk."

"You've got some nerve, Tyler Carson! You're the one with the courtroom manner and silver tongue. I wouldn't have gotten myself in this mess if I hadn't listened to you in the first place." She started to get up from the chair.

"If you know what's good for you, you'll stay where you are, Carly." His steely eyes pinned her to the back of the cushion. "I've put up with about all of the nonsense I'm going to. I don't relish chasing around after you in the middle of the night when we could both be in our own beds getting some much needed sleep. You chose the time and place, and by God, you'll have to live with it."

Carlisle listened to him as if she resented every word he spoke. "Nobody forced you to come after me," she pointed out.

"Yes, they did—you did, honey." Tyler gave an irritated laugh. "You can't believe for a minute that I would allow you to walk out of my life that easily. Now, I'm going to ask you one more time. What the hell is going on?"

Surprised by this outburst, Carlisle recoiled from him and then regained her composure. "I should think you would know the answer to that."

The man swallowed a deep breath of air. "Well, I don't," he confessed, running his fingers through the mop of unruly brown hair. "I realize getting caught in that storm yesterday was pretty rough on you, but I can't believe you would run away because of something like that."

"Chalk one up for you, Mr. Carson," she said flippantly. "The storm had nothing to do with it."

His voice was soft and cold when he spoke next. "Then why? What happened to the warm, loving woman I held in my arms last night and the night before? What happened to the woman who swore that she loved me?"

Carlisle bent her head and prayed for strength she did not have. "Maybe she changed her mind," she boldly lied.

He turned slowly, staring down into her eyes. "I don't believe you. And I'm not leaving this room until you say something that makes sense." He hurled himself into a chair and lit a cigarette, waiting for her to reply.

She gave him a quick look and hurriedly added, "All right then—I left because I didn't particularly care to be taken for a ride."

"Don't you have that turned around, sweetheart?" Tyler retorted, cutting her short. "I'm the one who's been taken for a ride."

"The only thing that's ever taken you for a ride is that big palomino of yours." She snorted.

He refused to acknowledge that comment. "I'm still waiting for you to say something that makes sense."

She cocked her head to one side and studied him. "I take back what I said before—you're a much better actor than I gave you credit for."

Tyler held her eyes a moment longer. "I have never acted with you, honey. I've never been anything but honest. And believe me, I'm paying for it in full."

"Then what about you and Maria Chavez?" Carlisle threw in his handsome face. "I suppose that's what you call being honest."

"Why do you insist upon bringing Maria into every conversation we have?" His impatience with her grew. "The girl means nothing to me beyond the fact she is the daughter of good friends of mine."

"Sure—and I suppose that little scene in the hall this afternoon was 'nothing,' too." Carlisle quickly clamped a hand over her mouth, realizing too late that she had given herself away.

A bright light went on in Tyler's eyes. "You were eavesdropping again, weren't you?" He put his head back and let out a surprised laugh. "Is *that* what this whole thing has been about?"

"I wasn't listening on purpose," she added in her own defense. "I was on my way to the kitchen for something to eat."

Tyler quit talking and rose to his feet. He placed a hand on either arm of her chair and leaned forward eagerly. "Oh, Carly—what hell you've put me and yourself through for no reason." He swooped down and claimed her lips in a tantalizing kiss that took her breath away.

"Don't think you can talk your way out of this one so easily, Tyler Carson!"

"Talking wasn't what I had in mind." He grinned, eyeing the bed beside them.

Carlisle jerked around to stare into his eyes with sudden comprehension. "Forget it!"

The man merely smiled and shrugged. "There isn't anything between Maria and me, honey. You've heard the expression you can 'catch more flies with honey than vinegar'? Well, that's what I was doing this afternoon. I didn't realize you were listening to that line of tripe I was handing her and believing every word."

Carlisle looked at him under skeptical brows. "I can't wait to hear the rest of this one," she scoffed.

Tyler's mouth drew into a tight thin line. "I'm perfectly serious about this, Carlisle. Maria had to learn once and for all that the only woman in my life is you. I had my suspicions from the start that she let you deliberately go off to Elizabethtown, knowing full well a storm was brewing. Her antics were getting dangerous. So I arranged for her to come over to Chula Vista this afternoon. When she arrived I played along with her until I got the truth. It's too bad you didn't hear the rest of our conversation. Suffice it to say, she won't be pulling any more tricks like that one. In fact, Maria has decided to attend a university in California this fall."

"Are you telling me the truth, Tyler?" Carlisle asked quietly, undoing her hand from his.

"I swear it's the truth!" he declared passionately.

"Well, I appreciate your coming by to tell me," she said, in a hoarse whisper. "Now if you don't mind, I have an early flight tomorrow and I need my sleep."

Tyler fell back a step as if she had slapped him across the face. "What do you mean you have an early flight tomorrow? I'm in love with you, Carly. I want you to come back to Chula Vista with me."

There was a great sadness in the woman's voice. "There's just no future for us, Tyler. You must see that, too. I-I think it would be best for both of us if we made a clean break now."

"You're in love with me. Dammit—I know you are!" he roared like a wounded lion. "The way you go all soft and pliable in my arms when I kiss you. The way your body arches to mine in hunger when we make love. God, we're so good together, Carlisle. You can't just throw that away!"

"It's not enough, Tyler." She choked back the tears. "Don't you understand that it's not enough for me?"

The man staggered backward until his knees hit the

edge of the mattress behind him. He slowly sank down and buried his head in his open hands dejectedly. For several minutes he seemed incapable of speech.

"I-I'm sorry . . ." Carlisle heard herself apologizing without knowing what she was apologizing for.

"Sorry, Carlisle? You can keep your lousy sorrow. I don't want it," he muttered bitterly.

"I'm not pitying you, Tyler. What I feel is for both of us—you and me," she tried to explain. "I-I wish it could have been different for us, that's all."

He finally raised his head and she was stunned by the expression of pain in his eyes. "I don't suppose you have anything to drink around here," he asked, moving his mouth with difficulty.

"I-I'm sorry. I had a cola but I'm afraid I drank it," she said sheepishly.

"Will you stop saying you're sorry all the time." Tyler's lips curled in a growl. "What I need to drink is something a hell of a lot stronger than a soft drink!"

Carlisle's eyes drained of vitality. "Oh—I'm sorry . . ."

The man gave her a scathing look that said far more than mere words. "So . . ." He sprang to his feet and began to pace the floor of the small motel room like a caged animal. "Where do we go from here? I suppose you intend to return to Denver, accept another assignment in one of the four corners of the world, and carry on with your life." He bit off the last word as he halted directly in front of Carlisle. His face was so close to hers she could make out the yellow darts in the pupils of his eyes. "And do you know where that leaves me?" Tyler demanded, his breath hot on her skin.

She could only shake her head. "N-no . . ." she finally murmured, half in fear.

"Then let me tell you, my *dear.*" He twisted the word purposely as he spoke, lacing it with undisguised sarcasm. Carlisle knew she was not going to like what Tyler seemed determined to say to her. His male pride had been dealt a tremendous blow and he was out to hurt something or someone in return. "I will be left in a house where everything I see or touch has been poisoned for me." There was an unmistakable tone of bitterness in his voice.

Carlisle's heart was thumping intolerably. "Oh, no, Tyler—why?" Her tone matched the despair of her countenance.

Holding her chin in his hand he looked down into her eyes. "Because every night when I climb those stairs I will have to walk by the room where we made love. I'll lie in my bed and wonder who is making love to you and curse the world because it isn't me." Then he kissed her, deeply, passionately, until they both felt the pain. He lifted his head and gave a husky laugh that failed to ring true. "You know, I've always felt so free in New Mexico. But right now it looks like one big prison."

"You can't live that way," she implored. "It isn't right."

"Then come back with me, Carlisle," he said, in his most persuasive voice.

She felt her heart shatter into a thousand tiny pieces and knew it would never be whole again. "I-I can't! Don't you see I can't live that way?" She put a palm against his chest, counting his heartbeats.

He straightened up and abruptly moved away from her. He dug his hands deep in the pockets of his jeans and stared vaguely at the print hanging over the bed. "Yeah . . . I guess I do see."

Carlisle was suddenly angry with him and the reason for it escaped her. "I thought I could handle having an affair with you, Tyler—but I can't! If I go back to Chula Vista with you now, it will hurt just that much more when we finally do part, only I won't have a shred of self-respect left to call my own." She glared up at him, a look of pure fury burning in her eyes. "You may think New Mexico will be your prison, but it won't matter where I go or what I do—none of it will mean a thing without you!" The words became strangled in her throat as she fought for breath. "I love you, Tyler. I'll always love you—but I can't go on being your mistress."

The man had stood strangely still during her tirade, as if he couldn't quite believe what he was hearing. Groping to recover his inner balance, he grated, "I don't want you for my mistress, Carlisle."

She looked up at him, uncomprehending. "You—you don't?"

Tyler hardly dared to breathe. "No, I don't! I want to marry you. I want you to be my wife."

She sat white and silent. "We n-never talked about marriage," she stammered.

"Dammit, woman, how could I? You made it clear from the beginning that your profession always came first. You told me yourself that you'd broken off with more than one man when he couldn't accept that." Tyler was on a pretty good tirade of his own. Then suddenly aware that he was shouting, he lowered his voice and continued. "I figured the best I could do was to keep on loving you the only way I knew how. Maybe during the time you were here building the dam you'd learn to feel the same way about this land as I do. Just maybe you would come to see it and me as your future."

"But I love New Mexico," Carlisle murmured, almost to herself.

"It wouldn't be enough though, would it?" he demanded ruthlessly. "I've racked my brain night and day trying to find a way. I won't ask you to give up being an engineer, honey. I'll take whatever I can get, even if it means only a few weeks a year with you."

The moment grew into a minute and then several minutes. "Y-you mean I could use Chula Vista as my home base?" she asked in a small firm voice.

"Yes!" Tyler said without reservation.

"No 'open' marriage!" she added vehemently.

"You'd better believe no open marriage," he reiterated possessively.

"Fortunately"—the woman gave a half-laugh—"I have a job to complete right in your vicinity, Mr. Tyler Carson. It should take all summer."

"Then we'll have one hell of a great summer," the man vowed, the strain starting to fade from his features. "It'll work out, Carly. I promise." Tyler drew her to him, wrapping his arms around her waist. "Don't ask me to like it when you have to go away on a job, but I will try to understand. I know now I can't live without you."

"I know the feeling," Carlisle murmured, slipping her hands up his chest to encircle his neck.

Their mouths met at last in an urgent confirmation that they had not really lost each other after all.

"Oh, God—I love you so much, Carly!" He groaned against her lips, his hands moving in a caress down her back to meld her hips to his, as hot metal melts into hot metal until it is one.

Carlisle felt herself go soft against him, recognizing the familiar languor that invaded her at his touch. How could she leave this man even for a night? she thought with anguish. There must be a way to have the best of both worlds. And she would find it, she vowed, as she gave herself up to the wild racing of her heart pressed to his.

She met the passionate demand of his mouth and hands with an equal force of her own as she opened up beneath him and took his breath for her own. Free now to express her love as she had never been before, Carlisle boldly unbuttoned Tyler's shirt and tossed it aside in imitation of his own earlier action. Her fingertips explored the muscled landscape of his chest and back as if he were one of the great wonders of the world. And when she found the belt buckle that cut between them and removed this obstacle from her path, the man shuddered in her arms.

The flimsy material of her nightgown presented no barriers to Tyler's intense search for each and every pulse point, a search that sent shivers of delight rippling along Carlisle's flesh. How quickly he had memorized the vulnerable points of her body. She found herself thrilling to his touch as never before. The full realization of their love set them both free.

He slipped the thin straps of her nightgown from her shoulders so his mouth and tongue and hands could savor and do equal honor to the spot beneath her ear, the tender sensitive skin of her shoulder where it met her neck, the rising mounds of her breasts that strained to be set free in their hunger for his touch.

Carlisle groaned her need and Tyler quickly raced to meet it, urging the top of her gown down around her waist. His head bent to tease the pink tips into an awareness of his caress. They grew and darkened under his loving attention as he caught one hard button between his teeth. The woman wanted this and yet so much more. Her own hands slipped inside the waistband of his jeans to anchor him to her so he would never let her go.

Their flesh was hot to the touch as they tried to light the fire of passion in each other. Tyler ran his hands through the long auburn strands as though he almost hoped to become permanently entangled in their fiery bonds. His breathing was labored as if he had run a great distance to reach her.

Then the man swept her up into his arms and carried her the short distance to the bed. He gently laid her down as if she were the most precious thing in the world to him. Then Tyler quickly divested himself of the remainder of his clothes and stretched out beside her. "I need you, Carly. Oh, how I need you!" he confessed in a hoarse whisper, gathering her in the circle of his embrace. "Not just tonight, but for all the nights to come."

"And I need you, Tyler," she just as quickly reassured him in ways of her own. "I don't know how I ever thought I could leave you."

Much as he tried, the man could not prevent the relief he felt from showing in his face. "Are you sure?"

Carlisle studied that face she loved so well—a face she knew better in some ways than her own. A face she had seen ablaze with passion and fear and anger—but most of all love. "Yes, I'm sure," she said, without hesitation. "I want the best of both worlds, Tyler, and I'm going to have them!"

"You're pretty pleased with yourself, aren't you, Miss Carlisle Scott soon-to-be Mrs. Tyler Carson?" The brown-gold eyes flickered almost humorously.

"I think I might keep the Carlisle Scott for business reasons," she muttered, in a pensive tone, drumming her fingertips against her lips.

"Would you mind hatching your business plans later, sweetheart? I had something else in mind right now." The man snuggled up to her in the most distracting way.

"Why, darling," she teased, even as she moved toward him. "You know business comes *before* pleasure," she murmured, tracing an erotic pattern on his body.

"Yes, my love," he murmured, as he nuzzled the tender pink tip of one ear.

Then Tyler was working his magic as only he could until Carlisle clung to him eagerly. "Well—perhaps we could make an exception just this once."

Silhouette Desire
15-Day Trial Offer

*A new romance series
that explores
contemporary relationships
in exciting detail*

Four Silhouette Desire romances, free for 15 days!
We'll send you four new Silhouette Desire romances
to look over for 15 days, absolutely free! If you decide
not to keep the books, return them and owe nothing.

Four books a month, free home delivery. If you like
Silhouette Desire romances as much as we think you
will, keep them and return your payment with the
invoice. Then we will send you four new books every
month to preview, just as soon as they are published.
You pay only for the books you decide to keep, and
you never pay postage and handling.

Coming Next Month

Velvet Touch by Stephanie James

Tawny, elegant Lacey Sheldon was determined to
cut loose from her librarian's past and find
liberation out west. This island paradise in Puget
Sound seemed the perfect place to begin . . . until
she met Holt Randolph. He said he didn't want
half a heart, and challenged her to gamble it
all in a blazing affair that would bring
her to her senses—and into his arms.

The Cowboy And The Lady by Diana Palmer

Jace had given Amanda her first taste of passion.
His silver eyes had held a forbidden fascination for
her, but at sixteen she'd been too inexperienced to
understand the fiery message in his searing kisses.
Now Amanda was ready to learn the lessons of
desire, and there was only one man who could
teach her—a man whose glittering gaze held
the secrets of her unhappy past and the
promise of a golden future.

Silhouette Desire

Coming Next Month

Come Back, My Love by Pamela Wallace

TV newsperson Toni Lawrence was on the fast track to fame when photographer Theo Chakaris swept her off her feet at the Royal Wedding. How had she abandoned herself to this adventurer? Storybook romances belonged to princes and princesses. She tried to forget, to bury herself in her work, but passion brought them together to recapture the glory of ecstasy.

Blanket Of Stars by Lorraine Valley

Greece was the perfect setting for adventure and romance. But for Glena Fielding it became more. This land she would call home. In Alex Andreas' dark eyes she saw a passion and a glory, a flame to light her senses and melt her resistance beneath the searing Greek sun. In his arms she became invincible as he led her to the stars.

YOU'LL BE SWEPT AWAY
WITH SILHOUETTE DESIRE

$1.75 each

1 ☐ CORPORATE AFFAIR
Stephanie James

2 ☐ LOVE'S SILVER WEB
Nicole Monet

3 ☐ WISE FOLLY
Rita Clay

4 ☐ KISS AND TELL
Suzanne Carey

5 ☐ WHEN LAST WE LOVED
Judith Baker

6 ☐ A FRENCHMAN'S KISS
Kathryn Mallory

7 ☐ NOT EVEN FOR LOVE
Erin St. Claire

8 ☐ MAKE NO PROMISES
Sherry Dee

9 ☐ MOMENT IN TIME
Suzanne Simms

10 ☐ WHENEVER I LOVE YOU
Alana Smith

Silhouette Desire

Now Available

Not Even For Love by Erin St. Claire

When a misunderstanding threatened to drive them apart, the memory of their passion drove Jordan to convince Reeves of the truth. His misty green eyes and sensual mouth had lifted her to peaks of ecstasy she could never forget.

Make No Promises by Sherry Dee

Even though Cassie was engaged to another man, she was instantly attracted to Steele Malone. He waged a passionate war on her senses, defying her emotions and lulling her body with primitive pleasures.

Moment In Time by Suzanne Simms

She knew Tyler expected a man to build his treasured dam, but Carly was a fully qualified civil engineer. What began as a battle of wills blazed anew in the Santa Fe sunset, a flashfire passion which consumed them both.

Whenever I Love You by Alana Smith

Diana Nolan was Treneau Cosmetics' new goddess of beauty. Paul Treneau was the boss who whisked her away to his Hawaiian paradise for "business." But she had ignited in him a spark of desire fated to burn out of control.